SECRETS AND DREAMS

Jean Ure

SECRETS AND DREAMS

HarperCollins *Children's Books*

First published in Great Britain by HarperCollins *Children's Books* 2015
HarperCollins *Children's Books* is a division of HarperCollins*Publishers* Ltd,
1 London Bridge Street
London SE1 9GF

Visit us on the web at
www.harpercollins.co.uk

1

Secrets and Dreams
Copyright © Jean Ure 2015

Jean Ure asserts the moral right to be identified as the author of this work.

ISBN 978-0-00-755395-2

Set in GillSans by Palimpsest Book Production Limited,
Falkirk, Stirlingshire

Printed and bound in England by
Clays Ltd, St Ives plc

For Ellie-May Lambourne

If Mum and Dad hadn't won the lottery, I would never have gone to boarding school.

If Gran hadn't given me her collection of Enid Blyton books, I would never even have *thought* of going to boarding school.

And if I hadn't caught the chicken pox from my dear little sister, I wouldn't have started a week late; and if I hadn't started a week late I might not have got tied up with Rachel and her problems.

Not that I realised straight away that Rachel had any problems. That came later. When we first met she just seemed a bit... well, different, I suppose. But I was different too! Nobody else's mum and dad had suddenly won the lottery and come into lots of money. We were both keeping secrets, I guess.

CHAPTER ONE

When Mum asked me and Natalie to sit down, saying she had something to tell us, we knew at once it had to be something exciting cos Mum's face was all scrunched and eager. But when she said that she and Dad had won the lottery we were, like, *WOW!* Well, I was like *wow*. Nat was more like punching the air and screaming.

"Now, just calm down," begged Mum. "I know it's cause for celebration but we don't want to go mad."

Too late! Nat was already going mad. Round and round the room, springing and leaping, and shouting out.

"We've won the lott'ry, we've won the lott'ry!"

I turned, wonderingly, to Mum.

"Are we rich?"

"Well, it's not a rollover," said Mum. "Hardly a drop in the ocean it'd be, to some folks. The Queen, for instance. But for me and your dad –" a big happy beam stretched across her face – "for me and your dad it'll make all the difference in the world. Well, for the whole family, obviously! I just meant that me and your dad won't have to struggle any more. And maybe – no promises! – we might be able to indulge you both just a little bit!"

"Does that mean I can have a dog?" cried Nat. "Oh, please, Mum, please! Say that I can!"

Nat had wanted a dog for as long as anyone could

remember. Mum had always said it wasn't possible, living in a small flat. But now we didn't have to. Now we could move! We could move anywhere we wanted. Even to one of the big expensive houses in the posh part of town. The ones Mum was always sighing over.

"What it must be like," she used to say, as we drove past in Dad's little old rattling van. "All that space!"

Oh, and I would be able to have my own room at long last. I was thirteen! I needed my privacy. It is no fun having to share with your little sister, especially one as messy as Nat. I'm sure by the time I was eleven I'd learnt to be a bit more considerate.

"Know what?" Nat suddenly flung out her arms, sending one of Mum's precious ornaments flying to the floor. "If we lived near a park we could have *two* dogs! Two's always better than one, cos one on its own gets lonely. And if you've got two it means you don't feel so bad going out and leaving them for a bit. It's actually quite *unkind*, just having one. I mean, if you stop to think about it—"

"Yes, yes, yes," said Mum, picking up her ornament. "I hear you! But before we get too carried away, let's just simmer down a bit. I told you, we're not going to go mad. Your dad and I have talked about this. We've decided that we should all choose one special thing we'd like to do, or have—"

"I've already decided!" Nat bounced back on to the sofa, next to me. "I want a dog!"

"Well, if that's what you've really set your heart on," said Mum. "But I'd like you both to go away and think about it. Seriously."

"You mean…" I said it slowly, my mind already buzzing with possibilities. "You mean, *whatever we want?*"

"Whatever you want," agreed Mum. "Though I'd rather you didn't ask for a wardrobe full of designer gear, or the latest techno-gadget. We'd like it to be something that's really important to you. Something that's going to last. Not just a spur-of-the-moment thing."

She told us both to go away and put some thought into it.

"And take your time! There's no rush."

"But I've already—" began Nat.

"I said, take your time," said Mum. "When you're both done thinking, we can have a family conference and see where we're at."

"Have you decided yet?" said Nat.

"No," I said. It had only been a few hours. "I'm still thinking."

"I've decided. I knew *immediately*. I don't need to think!"

"Well, I do," I said, "so if you'd just very kindly give me some peace and quiet, I might be able to get somewhere."

We were in our bedroom, Nat in her cubicle, me in mine. Mum had made curtains, which we could pull round our beds. We still had to share the wardrobe – *and* the dressing table, *and* the chest of drawers. We were supposed to have equal amounts of space, like half the wardrobe each, and half the dressing table, but Nat just had no idea of putting things away. Her clothes were everywhere, lying about in great festering heaps, along with empty crisp packets and chocolate wrappers. Really gross. Grown-ups are always going on about how *teenagers* turn their bedrooms into tips. Well, huh! They ought to start looking at eleven-year-olds, if you ask me.

"Hey, Zoe!" Nat's head came poking through the curtain.

I said, "*What?*"

"D'you think it's OK if we tell people?"

I wasn't too sure about that. "Dunno," I said. "Best ask Mum."

"Oh. OK." She sounded reluctant. "If I must." She was about to go off when her head came poking back in again. "You could always ask for skiing lessons."

"I don't want skiing lessons!"

Nat looked hurt. "You don't have to snap, I'm only

trying to be helpful! You wanted them last year. You and Sophie. You went on and on about them."

"That was when they had the Winter Olympics."

We'd watched them together. Me and Sophie. Sophie was my best friend ever! But last term she'd gone off to New Zealand with her mum and dad and I somehow didn't fancy the idea of learning to ski all by myself. It was *our* thing; mine and Sophie's. It wouldn't be the same without her. Come to think of it, nothing was the same without Sophie.

"So if you don't want skiing lessons…"

Omigod, I thought she'd gone!

"How about –" her face was all scrunched and excited – "how about asking for a pig?"

I said, "A *pig?*"

"A dear little pot-bellied piggy. They're so cute!"

"But I don't want a dear little pot-bellied piggy. You ask!"

"I can't. I've already decided. I'm just trying to give you some ideas!"

I said, "I can find my own ideas, thank you very much."

Nat sighed. She didn't actually *say*, "You are so mean at times," but it was probably what she was thinking. She stood there, on my side of the curtain, fingering her phone. Obviously dying to start spreading the news.

"I really don't see why I couldn't just tell Loo!"

I said, "Cos Loo's a bubblehead. And anyway, Mum's already said we don't want any publicity."

"But Loo's my best friend! I bet you'd have told Sophie."

Maybe I might have, but that was because Sophie and I never had secrets. And Sophie wasn't a bubblehead! She could be trusted.

"I wish you'd just go away," I said. "I'm trying to do some thinking here!"

"But I—"

"GO!"

Nat went mumbling off, leaving me to rack my brains. You would think, if your mum and dad gave you the chance to have *anything you want*, you would be spoilt for choice. Like, there would be just so many things clamouring for attention you'd find it hard to know which one to pick. Not so! All the possibilities that had been swirling about inside my head suddenly burst like soap bubbles the minute I seriously considered any of them. What did I really want? What would I really like? "Something important," Mum had said. Something that was going to last. I couldn't think of a single solitary thing!

I sat cross-legged on my bed, gazing at the posters pinned to the wall. Pop stars, rock groups. Jez Delaney … gorgeous Jez! The love of my life! Maybe I could talk Mum into getting me a ticket for his next gig? Except it was probably already sold out and, in any case, even I could see that going to a rock concert might not qualify as Something Important. Not in Mum's eyes.

So what did I want? What did I really *really* want? There had to be something!

My gaze fell upon Gran's old Enid Blyton books. They were all there, on the shelf. *The Twins at St Clare's, The Naughtiest Girl, Malory Towers,* et cetera. I had read them over and over, especially the school stories. I'd grown out of them now, of course, but I still couldn't bear to part with them. Mainly cos they'd belonged to Gran, but also cos I always used to feel that the characters were my friends. That I was there with them at St Clare's, or Malory Towers. It had been my dream to go to boarding school! I'd even begged Mum, when I was, like, nine or ten, to let me go to one. We hadn't been able to afford it then. But now that we had won the lottery…

Yessss! I bounced off the bed. I knew what I wanted to do!

"Right," said Dad. "Moment of truth!"

It was later that same day. Dad had come back from

work and we were all sitting round the kitchen table having what Dad called a *powwow*.

"Have you both had time to think?" said Mum.

"I didn't have to think," boasted Nat. "I already knew!"

"What about Zoe?"

I said, "Yes, I've decided."

"Well, that was quick," said Mum. "OK, if you're sure, let's get started. Your dad first!"

I know Dad was every bit as excited as the rest of us. He is just not the sort of person to show his emotions. But even he couldn't stop a big grin engulfing his face. He told us that he had already handed his notice in.

"Couldn't do it fast enough!"

Dad had never really cared for his job. He was always telling me and Nat how important it was, if you possibly could, to find work that gives you satisfaction.

"But he's not going to be a gentleman of leisure," said Mum. "Are you?"

She looked across at Dad like she was really proud

of him. Dad, suddenly going all bashful and un-Dad-like, agreed that he wasn't.

"Wouldn't suit me, sitting around doing nothing." He said he was going to carry on working, but not for the council. "For myself!"

"He's going to start up his own business," said Mum. "*Mr Bird, the Handyman.*"

"What do you reckon?" said Dad. "Catchy?"

"Brilliant," I said.

"We'll get a nice new van," said Mum, "have it all painted up."

"And a car," said Dad. "About time we had a proper car."

"Now that we're rich," said Nat.

Mum frowned.

I said, "That is *so* not cool!"

"Well, but we are," said Nat. "We *are*," she insisted, "aren't we?"

"I prefer to think of it as no longer being chronically hard up," said Mum.

Dad chuckled. "Tell them what you've decided on!"

Mum said that what she wanted was to move to a house – "Somewhere nice" – with lots of rooms and a large garden. No surprise there!

"Now ask me," said Nat. "Ask me what I want!"

"We know what you want," I said.

"No, you don't! I want a dog—"

"You already told us that."

"And a pony!"

She announced it with a triumphant flourish. Dad blinked, but even the pony wasn't all that much of a surprise. Two summers ago we'd gone on a camping holiday to Devon and Nat had done some riding at a local stable. We both had, but Nat had become, like, obsessed for a while. I thought she'd forgotten it. Obviously not!

Mum said that if Nat really and truly wanted her own pony then she supposed she could have one.

"So long as you'd be prepared to look after it properly. Not just leave it to other people."

Nat said, "Mum, of *course* I'd look after it!"

Nat is always saying *of course* she will do things and then never doing them, but I think in this case we all believed her. She is really into animals.

"Right," said Mum. "So what about Zoe? What has she decided?"

I took a breath. A really deep one. Right down to the bottom of my lungs.

"Well?" said Dad.

"*I'd like to go to boarding school!*"

The words came spurting out of me. It was the only way I could do it. All in a rush, before I got cold feet.

There was this long, shocked pause while they all gaped at me; then Dad said, "*Boarding* school?"

I appealed to Mum. "You know I always wanted to!"

"Well – yes," agreed Mum, sounding rather shaken. "I suppose you did."

"I did! I always did!"

"This is ridiculous," said Dad. "She can't go to boarding school!"

"She's mad," said Nat.

"You do realise," warned Mum, "that it wouldn't be like it is in Gran's books?"

"I know that," I said. I wasn't stupid! I could tell the difference between stories and real life. "Mum, I really do want to go!"

"But what about all your friends?" spluttered Dad.

"I'll just make more," I said.

I don't have any problems making friends; I'm what Mum calls "an easy mixer." I hadn't exactly been moping around since Sophie left. But there wasn't anyone *special*. No one that could replace Sophie. I was looking forward to meeting new people.

Dad was frowning at me like I was being really disloyal, but I think Mum understood how I felt. She knew how close me and Soph had been.

"Mum?" I said. "*Please?*"

"Well –" Mum turned to consult Dad – "I suppose, if she's genuinely serious about it?"

"I am!" I said. "I am!"

"We did promise," said Mum. "Anything they wanted."

"Within reason," muttered Dad.

I said, "Da-a-a-d!"

"A promise is a promise," urged Mum.

Dad shook his head.

"Dad, please," I begged.

There was a bit of a silence. Mum and I exchanged glances. Then Dad threw up his hands like, what can you do?

"All right, all right! I give in."

"Does that mean I can go?"

"Well, it seems your mum's in favour, so… I suppose the answer is yes."

Yay! Mum gave me this little secret wink. She can always manage to get round Dad!

"We'd better start looking for somewhere," she said. "It'll be no use trying for one of those places where you have to have your name put down at birth."

Eagerly I said, "I've been looking on the computer. I think I've already found one that would be OK. And it's not all that far away!" I'd purposely picked one that was quite close, cos I knew Mum wouldn't be happy if I couldn't get home occasionally. Maybe I wouldn't, either. "Shall I show you?" I said. "D'you want to come and see?"

"Why not?" said Mum. "No time like the present."

After that, everything happened really fast. Dad bought a smart new van and set himself up as *The Handyman.* Mum fell in love with a house just outside of town and almost before we knew it we were moving in there. Nat then dragged us all off to the nearest animal shelter and found an adorable Staffy pup, all rubbery and wrinkled, that she said she was going to call Lottie – "Short for lottery!" The pony was going to take a bit longer, but Nat said she didn't mind waiting, as it would give her a chance to do a bit of puppy training. Mum was pleased. She said, "It's really given her a sense of responsibility, having a pet to look after."

Even though I am not specially a dog person, I had to admit that Lottie was pretty cute. She had this funny little habit of licking your ears, getting her tongue really deep inside and slurping about. Once I would have thought it disgusting; now I just giggled. Nat, needless to say, was like totally besotted. She said she didn't know how I could bear to go away and not be there to see Lottie grow up.

I pointed out that I was only going to be away during the week. Mum had insisted on that. "I want you home at weekends!"

The school I'd found was called St Withburga, which Nat immediately started calling St Cheeseburga, like it was screamingly funny. I forgave her, though. I was just so excited! I couldn't wait to get there. The school hadn't been going all that long, so they still had places, plus they were only a short journey away, which made Mum happy. She and Dad took me down there to check it out, and even Dad had to admit that it seemed OK. High praise, coming from Dad!

"It's nice and small," said Mum. "I like that."

She added that it struck her as very funny, though, that I'd been complaining for years about having to share a bedroom with Nat and now here I was, choosing to share a dormitory with a bunch of total strangers!

I said that that was different. It was what you expected at boarding school.

Nat, who had come with us (simply to be nosy), told me for the hundredth time that I was mad.

"They'll be all snooty and look down on you."

"Why would they do that?" said Mum.

"Cos it's what they're like," said Nat. "Posh people!"

"She could be right," said Dad. He looked at me anxiously. "Are you sure about this, kiddo? You honestly want to come here?"

"I do," I said. "I'm really looking forward to it!"

So there it was, all settled. Me and Mum went into

Norwich to buy my uniform and various other bits and pieces that I was going to need, and that was it. I was ready! Just three weeks to go.

And *that* was when I caught the chicken pox.

CHAPTER TWO

It was the middle of September when I finally started at St With's (as I soon learnt to call it). I was a whole week late! I couldn't help thinking if there was anyone else that was new, they'd have made friends by now, which meant I'd be the odd one out. I told Nat that if she hadn't gone and breathed on me I might never have caught her rotten chicken pox. It was just an observation. She didn't have to get all uppity about it.

"Wasn't my fault," she said. "I didn't know it was the chicken pox!"

I said, "Well, considering you were covered in *spots*." Which she'd scratched. At least I hadn't done that.

"I meant at the *beginning*," she said. "At the *beginning* I didn't know. And anyway, you're not the only one starting a new school. It's just as bad for me."

"It was *your* chicken pox," I said. "And it's nowhere near as bad for you!" Nat was starting at secondary school. She'd still be with lots of her friends. "It's loads worse if it's boarding school."

"Well, you chose it," said Nat.

That was the point at which Mum came into the room. "Are you two at it *again*?" she said. "What's going on? You never used to fight like this. It's enough to make me wish we'd never won the wretched lottery!"

I couldn't believe Mum really meant that. She loved her new house with its big garden.

"I do hope," she said, "that you're not regretting this, Zoe?"

"I'm not!" I said.

I was just having a sudden attack of what Gran calls the collywobbles. Not even that, really. Just the odd flutter, like butterflies in my tummy.

Mum and Dad drove me down to St With's on a Sunday afternoon. Nat had to come with us on account of Mum thinking she was too young to be left on her own. We squabbled again in the car. Nat had found a new joke: instead of going to St Cheeseburga, I was now going to St Beefburga. She cackled uproariously as she said it. *Several times.* In the end I told her to shut up. She said, "You're not supposed to speak to me like that." I said I could speak to her how I liked, it was a free country. So then she said, "This is what happens when people go to posh schools – they get all big-headed."

"Talking about big heads," I said, "you'd just better be careful you don't fall off your *pony*, when you get one, and knock all your brains out! Not," I added, "that you have much in the way of brains to begin with. It's mostly just sawdust."

She then yelled, "*Beefburga!*" in a mindless kind of way, but before I could think of a suitable retort Dad told us both to be quiet, he was sick of the sound of our voices, while Mum said that if this was what having a bit of money did to us she'd almost be tempted to give our share to charity. She said Nat didn't deserve a pony and I didn't deserve to go to boarding school. Just for a moment I felt like saying, *All right, then, I won't!*

The butterflies were flapping like crazy, all swooping and swarming. To be honest, if Dad had said, "Let's just forget about it and go home," I'd have been secretly relieved.

Miss Latimer, the Head of Boarding, was there to meet us when we arrived, sweeping up the drive in Dad's new car. The first new car we'd ever had!

Miss Latimer said, "Zoe! I'm so glad you could make

it at last." She said it like she really meant it, like she'd almost been counting the days till I could come. I immediately felt a whole lot better. The butterflies had settled down and I couldn't wait to get up to the dorm and start arranging my things.

Dad wanted to carry my bags up there, but Miss Latimer said it was all right, Mr Bracey would do that. I thought Mr Bracey must be a teacher, and I guess so did Dad cos he said, "No, no, that's not necessary! I can do it." But then Mr Bracey appeared and simply picked up the bags and went off with them, leaving Dad standing there. It was ages before I discovered that Mr Bracey was the man who did things around the school. He was like Dad! Dad was *The* Handyman, Mr Bracey was the *school* handyman.

Mum was eager to come and help me unpack, but I told her I could do it myself.

"Are you sure?" said Mum, sounding a bit worried. It was like suddenly she didn't want to go off and leave me there.

I said, "Honestly, Mum! I can manage."

I so didn't want Nat trailing upstairs with us, making her stupid Beefburga jokes and ruining everything before I'd even started!

"We'll take good care of her," said Miss Latimer. "Don't worry."

I waved goodbye quite cheerfully to Mum and Dad and followed Miss Latimer into Homestead House. Homestead was where us seniors lived. The juniors were in the Elms. All the dormitories were named after flowers. Year Eights were Buttercup and Daisy, which was another reason I hadn't wanted Nat coming upstairs with us. She'd already gone off into peals of insane cackles about it. She kept spluttering, "*Butter*cups! *Dais*ies!" When Mum asked her what she found so funny she just cackled even harder.

"Personally I think it's nice they have pretty names," said Mum.

So did I! I didn't care *what* Nat thought.

I was in Daisy, which meant I had a cute little

lazy-daisy badge to pin on my sweater. There were six of us in there, three up one end of the dorm and three at the other, with a folding door in between. The Buttercups were further down the hall. There were also, Miss Latimer told me, six day girls, but of course they weren't in school on a Sunday. She said the other Daisies had gone off on a school trip, except for someone called Fawn, who had gone home for the weekend.

I was a bit alarmed at the thought of the unknown Fawn. What kind of a name was Fawn? It sounded like a posh person's name! Maybe my annoying little sister was right, and all the other girls would be smart and snobby and look down on me. I found that the collywobbles had suddenly come back.

"In case you're worrying about being the only new girl," said Miss Latimer, leading the way along the passage, "you're not alone. Rachel's also new. She arrived just a few minutes ago."

Miss Latimer tapped at the door, and paused a second

before opening it. I was well impressed! I am more used to people just barging in. Well, when I say "people", of course, I mean Nat. She'd *never* learnt to ask if she could come into my bit of bedroom.

"Here you are," said Miss Latimer.

A girl was standing at the window, leaning out at a perilous angle. She sprang round, her face lighting up. She seemed really pleased to see me.

"Rachel, this is Zoe Bird that I was telling you about. Zoe, this is Rachel Lindgren. The others are off on a school trip. They should be back in about half an hour, so they'll bring you down to tea. In the meantime, you know where to find me if you want me?"

Rachel beamed and said, "Yes!"

"Good. In that case, I'll leave you to get on with things."

I waited till Miss Latimer had gone, then said, "*I don't know where to find her.*"

"In her room," said Rachel. "At the end of the corridor." She bounced on to her bed and sat there, swinging her legs. "I've had the chicken pox," she said.

"Really?" I said. "Snap!"

Rachel giggled. She said, "*Snap?*"

"I've had it too! My sister gave it to me."

Rachel giggled again. "On purpose?"

Darkly I said, "I wouldn't be surprised. But I didn't scratch! Did you?"

"No, cos my auntie told me it would leave marks. Why did you say 'snap'?"

"Well – you know! Like the card game? When you say 'snap' if you both put down the same card?"

I thought everyone must have played Snap at one time or another. But Rachel obviously hadn't. She was looking at me, with her brow furrowed.

"Are you Swedish?" I said.

If she was Swedish, then maybe that would account for it. Maybe in Sweden they didn't play Snap. The reason I thought she might be was partly cos she looked a bit Swedish, like very pale with hair that was almost white, and partly cos of her name: Lindgren. I was quite proud of knowing that Lindgren was a Swedish name. I reckon not everyone would have done. I only knew cos a lady that used to live in our road had been called that and she came from Sweden. But the minute I asked the question I was covered in embarrassment and thought maybe I shouldn't have. Sometimes it is considered rude to ask people where they come from. I once asked a girl at my old school where she came from, thinking she would say, like, the West Indies or somewhere, and she said she came from Essex. She was quite cross about it, though I was only trying to be friendly.

Fortunately Rachel didn't seem to mind. She said that she wasn't Swedish but her granddad had been.

"He was called Lindgren. That's why I am." And then she gave this shriek of laughter and cried, "Yoordgubba!" Well, that was what it sounded like. I only discovered later that it was spelt "Jordgubbe". Rachel said it was Swedish for strawberry.

"And *toalettpapper* is toilet paper!"

I didn't quite know what to say to that. "So do you speak Swedish?" I said.

She giggled again. She seemed to do a lot of giggling.

"*Hey*," she said. "That's 'hello'. *Hey!*" She held out her hand. She obviously wanted me to take it even though I'd already started to unpack and had my arms full of clothes. "Say it!"

Obediently I said, "*Hey*."

"There," said Rachel. "Now you know as much as I do! Except for *tack*. That means 'thank you'."

She picked up a pair of my socks that had rolled on to the floor.

Solemnly I said, "*Tack*." Little had I thought I would be in the dorm having a Swedish lesson the minute I arrived. Maybe chicken pox would prove to be a blessing in disguise? I'd made a friend already!

"Shall we stick together?" said Rachel. She sat, cross-legged, on her bed.

"Yes, let's," I said. "I've never been to boarding school before, have you?"

Rachel said, "No, but I know what to expect… I've read the books!"

"What, the leaflets?" I said. "The stuff they send you?"

"No!" She gave a great swoop of laughter. "The boarding-school books."

"Oh! You mean, like…"

"*The Naughtiest Girl in the School, Claudine at St Clare's*—"

This time, I was the one that giggled. "Snap again!" I said. "Me too! Only I don't think it's quite the same these days."

"That's what my auntie says. She says they're like really old-fashioned? But it's still going to be fun! I'm really looking forward to it. Midnight feasts and climbing out of the dorm at night… That's why I was looking out of the window! To see if there's an apple tree."

In spite of myself, I said, "Is there?"

"No, worse luck, but you can always make a ladder by tying pairs of tights together."

"Tight ropes!" I said. Quite clever, I thought. I waited for Rachel to giggle, but she just nodded, very earnestly.

"It's what they did in one book. Or of course you can climb down a drainpipe if you're brave enough."

"Or a fire escape," I said. "Or even a real rope, if you happen to have one."

I was being funny – sort of – but Rachel appeared to be taking it quite seriously. She agreed that a real rope would be best.

"Like a clothes line, or something."

I gazed at her, doubtfully. Did she really think we were going to have midnight feasts and go swarming out of the window on the ends of clothes lines?

I started to set out my photographs on top of my bedside table. I had one of Mum and Dad; one of Mum, Dad and Nat; and one of Nat with Lottie.

"Oh, cute!" squealed Rachel.

"I hope you mean Lottie and not Nat," I said.

"Which one's Lottie?"

"She's the dog. Nat's my sister."

"The one that gave you chicken pox?"

I said, "Yes. She breathed on me."

"Yeeurgh!" Rachel gave an exaggerated shudder. "That's gross!"

"She *is* gross." I glanced across at Rachel's cabinet. "Don't you have any photos?" I said.

Rachel put a finger to her mouth, like I'd caught her out in some sort of crime. "I didn't think."

"You ought to have some of your family. Your mum and dad."

"I haven't got a mum," said Rachel. "She died."

Omigod! It was one of those moments. I didn't know where to put myself.

"It's all right," said Rachel. "I never actually knew her."

She pushed her hair behind her ears. It was bright silver, very fine and wispy. Mine is like a doormat. One of those fierce brown bristly ones.

"It was in childbirth, you see."

I am not very often at a loss for words, but I honestly couldn't think what to say. I just gulped and went, "Oh." I wondered, if she didn't have a mum, who Rachel lived with. Whether it was her dad, or her auntie that she'd mentioned. I didn't like to ask, though, in case it seemed like prying. You can't be too nosy when you've only just met someone.

From somewhere in the building we heard the sound of doors opening and closing, followed by girls' voices and footsteps along the corridor.

"That'll be the others come back," I said.

We shot these glances at each other. Not exactly nervous, but maybe just a tiny bit apprehensive. We were the new girls! What were they going to make of us?

"We will be best friends," said Rachel, "won't we?"

I wasn't sure you could become best friends just like that, but I said yes all the same. Rachel gave me this big happy smile, showing all her teeth, and I smiled back. She was a bit odd, but I did like her.

The door suddenly flew open – no knocking, this time – and four girls came bursting in. They stopped at the sight of me and Rachel. One girl said, "Oops! Sorry. Didn't know you'd arrived. You must be Zoe and Rachel?"

Rachel giggled. I was beginning to think it must be some kind of nervous affliction, the way she kept doing it. The girl introduced herself as Fawn Grainger. She was obviously posh, like the way she spoke and everything, but she didn't seem stuck-up. She seemed quite friendly. She introduced the others as Dodie Wang, Tabitha Rose and Chantelle Adebayo. They seemed quite friendly too. Such a relief! I might have guessed Nat didn't know what she was talking about.

Fawn said, "Tab's sleeping up your end. We banished her, cos she snores. I know it's not fair, but we had to put up with her all last term."

Rachel giggled. Again. She said, "That's all right, my gran snores. She snores so much she makes the walls shake."

"This one buzzes," said Fawn. "It's like sleeping next to a giant bee."

After I'd finished unpacking, and everyone had looked at my photos and cooed over Lottie, we went down to tea, which was served in the refectory, in the main building next door. Us Daisies sat at our own table.

"Those are the Buttercups," said Fawn. "Over there. I'll introduce you afterwards."

Fawn was the class representative on the school council. She was obviously a natural leader, though she didn't strike me as being particularly bossy. She was just one of those people that everybody is happy to follow. Partly, I thought, it was the way she looked. She was more than just ordinarily pretty. She had a very delicate, heart-shaped face (I have *always* wished I could have a heart-shaped face; mine is more kind of square) and these great violet eyes with long sweeping lashes. Absolutely stunning!

The other three, I was glad to note, were more like normal ordinary human beings. Tabitha was quite plump and pillowy. I thought she looked like a comfortable sort of person. I reckoned she must be good-natured, cos she hadn't seemed to mind when Fawn had said about her snoring. Dodie was a tiny little spidery thing with a sweet little blob of a nose – something else I'd always wished for! Chantelle could almost have been a model, being very tall and slim, except her face was a bit too round. Models always look as if they're half starved.

For tea there were big plates of bread and butter – masses of it! – and various pots of jam. Rachel picked up one of the pots and waved it at me.

"Look," she said. "*Jordgubbe!*"

"Oh," I cried, "*jordgubbe* jam!"

We both giggled at that.

"'Yord' *what?*" said Tabitha.

"*Gubbe*," I said. "It's Swedish for strawberry."

"And *toalettpapper*," added Rachel, "is toilet paper."

I did think that perhaps that was a bit more information than we needed, at least at the tea table, but Rachel was beaming and seemed pleased with herself.

"What are your nicknames?" she said.

"Nicknames?"

They all looked blank. Rachel shrieked. "You've got to have nicknames!"

"Why?" said Dodie.

"Cos it's what people have!"

I couldn't imagine where Rachel had got that idea from. I didn't specially remember anyone having nicknames in Gran's Enid Blyton books.

"Chantelle is sometimes called Ellie," said Dodie, sounding rather doubtful. "And Tabitha's Tabs. Is that what you mean?"

"No!" Rachel shook her head. "They're just shortenings. I can't *believe* you don't have nicknames!"

"What sort of nicknames?" said Fawn.

"Well, like, you could be… Baby, for instance."

"*Baby?*" Fawn was staring at her with a kind of horrified fascination. "Why 'Baby'?"

Rachel gave one of her great swooping peals of laughter. "Cos a fawn's a baby animal!"

Fawn said, "I see."

"You have to be a bit inventive," said Rachel. "It's supposed to be fun!"

"So what's her nickname?" Fawn nodded towards me.

"Oh, she's Robin!"

I blinked. Why Robin? Chantelle asked the same question.

"Zoe *Bird*?" said Rachel.

"But why. Robin? Why not Albatross?"

"Or Wood Pigeon," said Dodie.

"Or Pelican."

"Or Budgerigar."

Rachel gave a happy hoot of laughter. "You can't call someone *Budgerigar*."

"You could call them Budgie," said Fawn.

I could see that Rachel was turning this over in her mind. Earnestly, as we left the refectory, she said, "Which would you rather be? Robin, or Budgie?"

"Not sure I really want to be either," I said.

"OK." Rachel nodded. "I'll try to think of something else."

"What about you?" I said. "What's your nickname?"

"Haven't got one," said Rachel.

"What were you at your old school?"

Her eyes slid away from me. "Just Rachel."

"I was just Zoe," I said. "We didn't have nicknames."

"That's cos it wasn't a boarding school."

"Oh. Well! In that case," I said, "you'll have to invent one for yourself."

"You can't invent your own nickname!" She said it like I should have known. "Other people do it for you. If you're popular enough."

Fawn came up to me later. "Did you and Rachel already know each other?" she said. "Were you at the same school, or something?"

I told her that we'd only just met, that afternoon. She seemed surprised.

"We thought you must already know each other. She's strange, isn't she?"

She was a bit, but I did quite like her. And I had agreed that we'd be friends.

Hurriedly, Fawn said, "Not that there's anything wrong with being strange! Last year we had this girl that used to keep bursting into song all the time. Like in the middle of class. It would suddenly come to her, and she'd just open her mouth and start singing. Now she's got a scholarship to study music. Turns out she's some kind of genius. Like Mozart, or something."

I said, "You think Rachel might be a genius?"

"Might be," said Fawn. "You never know. Anyway —" she slid her arm cosily through mine — "it's fun having new people in the dorm. And if one of you *did* happen to be a genius it would be really cool! At least it would get us one up on those Buttercups. They think *way* too much of themselves." She squeezed my arm. "I'm so glad you're a Daisy! I'm sure you're going to fit in perfectly."

I beamed. I couldn't help it! So much for Nat saying how everyone would be all snobby and look down on me.

"What about Rachel?" I said. I didn't want to sound too anxious, but if she and I were going to be friends it was important we should both fit in. Not just me.

"Oh, she'll be all right," said Fawn. "We don't mind if someone's a bit odd. It's better than being dull and boring!"

I certainly didn't think Rachel was likely to be that.

CHAPTER THREE

By Friday I was feeling so settled I almost didn't want to have to pack my bag and go home. I'd found a new friend in Rachel, and Fawn and the others had gone out of their way to make us both feel welcome. Even when they'd discovered that Rachel had never played netball before, they didn't roll their eyes or grow impatient when she messed up the game. Miss Simon, who took us for PE, said, "Don't worry, Rachel, you'll soon get the hang of it." But even when she didn't – when she *kept* trying to run with the ball or throw it madly in the wrong direction – they were all quite nice about it. Even Chantelle, who was sports crazy, and Fawn, who was so competitive. When two of the idiotic Buttercups started cackling, they turned on them quite savagely.

"*Such* bad manners," said Fawn.

"Pathetic," said Chantelle.

I was so glad they'd stuck up for Rachel! Especially Fawn. I'd already worked out that there was this massive rivalry between the two dorms, and that Fawn took it really seriously. She hated it when the Daisies were made to look ridiculous, so I thought it was specially good of her to leap to Rachel's defence. In spite of sometimes being a bit full of her own importance, she obviously had a sense of fair play.

With everything working out so well it was quite a wrench to tear myself away. Of course, I was looking forward to seeing Mum and Dad again, even to seeing Nat, and to telling them all about it, but I couldn't help feeling like I was missing out, going off and leaving everyone else behind to enjoy themselves. How could anybody bear to be a day girl? Not me!

Rachel was the only other one from Daisy dorm who wasn't staying on. Fawn had gone home last weekend, but she said she only did it occasionally.

"Like, if my gran's visiting, or something. It's more fun being here with the others."

A whole bunch of us was dropped off at the station. Dad had wanted to come and pick me up, but I'd begged to be allowed to use the train. It felt more independent, plus it meant I could be with Rachel. It turned out she lived just three stops further down the line from me.

"I'm really going to see if I can board full-time next term," I said. "I think I'll probably be able to talk Mum round, but Dad's funny. He didn't really want me to come to boarding school at all. He'd prefer it if I was just a Day." I didn't add that Dad would actually prefer it if I hadn't gone to St With's in the first place. One of my grans has always said that Dad has a chip on his shoulder. I wouldn't have wanted Rachel thinking that.

"How about your dad?" I said. "Or is he the one that decided?"

I was hoping she might be prompted to tell me something about herself. I couldn't help being curious. I still didn't know who she lived with – whether it was her dad, or her gran, or her auntie that she sometimes talked about. I didn't know where she'd been to school, or anything at all, really. She was eager to talk about most things – just not about herself.

So when I asked the question, thinking I was being very clever and cunning, I wasn't terribly surprised when she gave one of her great cascades of giggles and said, "It was me that chose!" It wasn't a proper answer, in fact it wasn't really an answer at all, but I didn't like to push. I know sometimes I can seem a bit nosy. A bit what Mum calls *intrusive*. But I did find it difficult! I think it is only natural to want to know things about people, especially if they are supposed to be your friend. Your *best* friend.

"Honestly," I said, "my dad's like a mother hen. He doesn't even like me taking the train! He wanted to come and pick me up. Of course it might just be cos he's got this new car and it's any excuse to go for a drive. That's what Mum says. How about yours?"

I couldn't help trying! But Rachel just giggled and said, "I like being on the train."

Again, it wasn't an *answer*. I asked her if anyone was meeting her at the station, and she said her auntie. I didn't even know her auntie's name. It was always just "my auntie".

"So what about when we go to the theatre?" I said.

In a fortnight's time the whole of our year was being taken to see a production of *A Midsummer Night's Dream*, which was the play we were doing in class. The bus was going to bring us all back to school afterwards, which meant Dad could always drive over and collect me if he really wanted, but I reckoned Mum would stick up for me if I pleaded to stay overnight at school and come home on Saturday.

I said this to Rachel. "It would be fun if we could both stay over! Do you think they'd let you?"

Her eyes did that thing where they shifted away. "I'm not sure if I'll be able to come."

Not come to the theatre? "Oh, but you've got to!" I said. "Everybody else is."

She was silent. She was hardly ever silent. Normally she was just as much a chatterbox as I am. Sometimes even more so, especially in the dorm after lights out. You'd be lying there trying to sleep and Rachel would be propped on her elbow talking at you in the darkness. It was worse than Tabs's snoring. The other night Fawn had yelled at her to "Just button it!" But then other times, like now, she'd totally clam up.

I wondered if it would be rude to ask her why she might not be able to come. Sometimes, at my old school, people hadn't been able to go on school trips because their mums and dads couldn't afford it. Once in Year Seven there'd been a weekend in France and it was my mum and dad that hadn't been able to afford it. Maybe Rachel was on some kind of scholarship and her dad, or whoever it was, didn't have enough money to pay for extras. In which case it would *definitely* be rude of me to ask.

I contented myself with reminding her that she would have to decide soon. She said, "Yes, I know, it's just—"

Too late! We had already pulled into the station and I could see Dad and Nat waiting for me on the platform. If only Rachel had got off before me instead of after, I might have had a glimpse of her mysterious auntie.

"Ask!" I said, as I jumped off the train.

Rachel nodded. "I will. I really want to come!"

Dad and Nat had spotted me. "There she is!" cried Dad.

"Back from St Beef's!" That, needless to say, was Nat.

"Enough with the Beef's," I said, giving her a shove.

Nat pulled a face. "So what's it like? Is it like Enid Blyton? Are they all posh?"

"Hold your horses," said Dad, "she's only just got here! She can tell us all about it when we're back home."

"Mum's made a special tea," said Nat, "just for you! She's done chocolate cake cos she knows it's your favourite. And pizza! It's not really healthy, chocolate cake and pizza all in the same meal, but Mum said just for once. I s'pose at St Beef's you have caviar and stuff."

"Yeah, that's a favourite," I said. "But then for tea we have bread and marge."

"*Marge?* Ugh! Yuck!"

"Plain and wholesome," said Mum, when Nat told her about it.

"You'd think they could come up with something a bit better," grumbled Dad. "I'm not paying all that money for my daughter to eat bread and marge!"

"Oh, Dad, it's bread and butter," I said. "And we have—"

I was going to say that we had *jordgubbe* jam to put on it, but Nat got in ahead of me.

"They have *caviar* for dinner!"

"Believe that and you'll believe anything," said Mum.

"No," said Nat. "She said!"

"She's pulling your leg. Lottie, get down, there's a good girl."

"Lottie's house-trained." Nat announced it, proudly. "She hasn't done anything indoors for ages."

Lottie wagged her tail so hard her whole body shook. She was still all rubbery and puppyish. I have to admit, Nat is really good with animals. She just has this irritating habit of totally annoying me! Like now.

"Who was that girl?" she said. "The one you waved goodbye to?"

"That was Rachel," I said. "She's in my dorm."

"She looks peculiar."

You see what I mean? Just, like, totally *annoying*.

"How does she look peculiar?" said Mum, sounding a bit annoyed herself. She knew about Rachel, cos I'd told her on the phone. She'd been pleased to hear that I'd already made a friend. "What's peculiar about her?"

"She's got white hair," said Nat.

"That's because she's Swedish!" I snapped.

Mum told me later that I shouldn't let Nat wind me up.

"Truth to tell, she's a bit resentful of you being at boarding school. I know it sounds silly, when it was her choice to have Lottie, and we're buying her a pony, but I think she's secretly scared you'll... how can I put it? Decide we're not good enough?"

I said, "Mum!" That was ridiculous.

"It's your dad as well," said Mum. "He's a bit of a worryguts. Give them time, they'll get over it. Tell me about Rachel! Does she live round here?"

I said that she lived just three stops further down the line.

"That's nice! So you could always visit each other if you wanted? Like in the holidays?"

"I suppose so," I said.

Mum must have detected a slight note of doubt in my voice. She said, "No?"

"Well… maybe."

"You're not that friendly with her?"

"I am! It's just… I don't know all that much about her. She never says anything."

"Give her a chance! You've only known each other a week," said Mum.

"Yes, but she knows about me. She knows about you and Dad, and Nat and Lottie. I've got photos by my bed! She hasn't got any. She did tell me her mum died when she was born, but I don't know where her dad is. I don't even know if she's got a dad. She never mentions him."

"It could be something she feels sensitive about," said Mum. "Not everyone pours out their heart and soul like you do! I'm sure she'll tell you in her own good time. Don't rush her."

I said, "I'm not! And I do like her. I really do!" She was very good-natured. Always giggly and happy and eager to be friends. And she was funny! She made people laugh. Except that thinking about it, maybe that was the problem. People didn't laugh because she was witty or clever but because she kept saying things, and doing things, that were kind of... well! A bit silly. A bit *childish*. That was why they laughed. And all the giggling and the eagerness to be friends – it was way over the top. To be honest, I sometimes found it embarrassing.

"Anyway," said Mum, "it's good that you've got someone. It's never easy finding your feet with a bunch of people who've already been together for a while."

"No, but they're all really nice," I said. "Not a bit snooty."

Not even the great Fawn Grainger that everyone looked up to. In spite of being rather grand, she was perfectly friendly; just as willing as the others to include me in things. I already felt like they'd accepted me as one of the group. They'd accepted Rachel too, in spite of her odd ways. My only slight worry was, how long could it last? How long would they go on making excuses for her? I'd said I'd be her friend, and I *was* her friend, but just now and again, when I saw Fawn and the others exchange looks, I couldn't help worrying that she might be going to hold me back. I know that is a totally horrible thing to say but it is the truth.

I didn't mention any of this to Mum, of course. She might go and tell Dad and then Dad would be like *I told you so.* "I told you she'd regret it!"

But I wasn't regretting it. Not one little bit! Just the

opposite! I was so eager to get back that instead of waiting till Monday I asked Mum if I could go on Sunday afternoon. She laughed and said, "Had enough of us already?"

"Mum," I said, "no! It's not that. It's—"

"Just that you want to be with your friends. It's all right, don't worry! I'm glad you're enjoying yourself. But I'll tell you what… you'd better let your dad drive you! That'll make him happy."

I got back to school to find Fawn and the others in the dorm getting ready for supper. Rachel hadn't yet arrived.

"Next term," I said, "I am *definitely* going to ask if I can board full-time."

"Yes, you should," said Fawn. "Then you'll properly be one of us."

I was so pleased to hear her say that!

Nobody asked me where Rachel was, and I am ashamed to admit that I was a little bit relieved. At least it showed they didn't think we were permanently glued together.

Rachel arrived just as we were on our way down to supper. Her face broke into this big soppy beam as she saw us. She came galumphing up the stairs with her arms flying out, almost poking a passing Buttercup in the eye.

"I'm happy," she cried. "I'm so happy, I'm so happy!"

"I'm glad someone is," said the Buttercup, sourly. Her name was Dana Phillips and she was quite bad-tempered at the best of times, though I can see that having a flying finger suddenly stab you in the eye would be enough to make anyone cross.

"Sorry, sorry!" Rachel's face was all lit up and radiant. "I'm just so happy! I can come! I can stay overnight! Hooray!" And then she gave this loud theatrical gasp and said, "Oh my gosh, crikey, is that the second bell? I must hurry!" And she galloped on, up the stairs.

There was a pause.

Tabs said, "'Oh my gosh, *crikey*'? Where's she get that from?"

"And what," asked Chantelle, "is she happy about?"

I said, "Coming on the theatre trip, I *think*."

Fawn caught up with me as I went ahead down the stairs.

"I know Rachel's your friend," she said, "but she really is quite loopy!"

CHAPTER FOUR

"*Seriously* weird."

We were wandering outside in the sunshine during lunch break, talking about Rachel. Well, the others were talking about Rachel; I was mostly just listening. I kept thinking, *I'm her friend. I should say something!* But what could I say? I couldn't say she wasn't weird, cos she absolutely was. On the other hand, nobody was being nasty about her. If they'd been nasty I would have spoken up. But all they were doing was just saying: Rachel was seriously weird.

"Know what she said the other day?" said Amy, in tones of what seemed to be genuine puzzlement. "She said, when were we going to have our midnight feast?"

"I know!" shrieked Chantelle. "She said that to me!"

"She wanted to know what she should bring."

"Sardines and condensed milk," said Chantelle. "That's what she suggested. She said we could dip the sardines in the condensed milk."

"Ugh, yuck!" said Tabs.

"Pur-*lease*," said Fawn.

"Where does she get these ideas?"

They all turned to me, like I could shed some light.

"Out of books, maybe?" I said.

"What books?" said Tabs. "I've never read any books where they eat sardines and condensed milk!"

"Old-fashioned books?"

"*She's* a bit old-fashioned," said Fawn, "when you come to think about it."

We all fell solemnly silent as we thought about it.

"Where is she right now, anyway?" said Tabs.

"Having an IT lesson," I said.

Rachel had three extra IT lessons a week. To begin with I'd thought maybe she was some kind of genius whizz-kid working on a program that was going to take the world by storm and that she couldn't be lumped in with the rest of us for fear we'd hold her back, but it seemed it was just the opposite. She actually didn't know the first thing about computers. She didn't even know how to switch one on!

"Where's she been living?" said Charlotte. She said it in tones of wonderment rather than irritation. "Under a stone, or what?"

They were all looking at me again. I shook my head.

"I mean, everybody does IT these days," said Tabs. "Even babies."

"Yes! Where did she go to school?" said Fawn. "Have you ever asked her?"

As a matter of fact I had, but she'd just giggled and said, "Somewhere!"

"She is so strange," said Amy.

"I think you should ask her," said Fawn.

"Why me?" I said.

"Well, you're more her friend than we are."

"Not specially," I said. "It's only cos we both started at the same time."

It was! I refused to feel guilty. If we hadn't both had the chicken pox and arrived late, I probably wouldn't ever have become friends with Rachel in the first place. It was her idea, not mine! Being friends, I mean. I'd just agreed cos it would have been ungracious to say no.

"Here she is," said Tabs.

Rachel came skipping towards us like an overgrown elf, waving and calling out: "Yoo-hoo!" The others exchanged glances. Chantelle rolled her eyes. A group of Year Sevens parted company to let her through. A couple of them sniggered.

"Omigod," said Fawn. "Look at the state of her!"

We'd had hockey first period before lunch, with a morning mist still hovering over the field, and Rachel's hair, which had started the day all bunched up in curls, was now hanging limply.

"Why does she *do* it?" wondered Chantelle.

She had this habit, every night, of winding her hair into pink plastic rollers, all fiercely bristled, so that she looked like a porcupine lying in bed. Sometimes one of the rollers would get loose in the night and then there would be a length of hair that hung straight down, while all the rest was frizzed up. Even when disaster didn't strike during the night, it only needed a spot of drizzle or damp weather to undo all the good work.

"Hi, guys!" Rachel came skittering up to us, her face split almost in two with its usual big beam. She was always so happy! And she always greeted you like she hadn't seen you for months, instead of just a few hours. A bit like Lottie, I couldn't help thinking.

I really hoped Fawn and Chantelle weren't going to mention her hair; it would be so humiliating for her. I find it bad enough when mine sticks up like a wire brush, but at least I can beat it back down or put a clip in it. Rachel's was hanging about in shreds, like a tattered curtain, and she had to spend the rest of the day with it like that.

"*There* you are," said Fawn.

"You found us," said Amy.

"Yes!" Rachel did a little twizzle. I did wish she wouldn't! It looked a bit… well, a bit daft, to be honest. "What are you talking about? Anything interesting?"

I saw Fawn flick a glance towards Chantelle. *Please don't*, I thought. *Please don't!*

I needn't have worried. It's true that Fawn can sometimes be a bit critical, and Chantelle quite blunt and in-your-face, but they are not purposely mean. And Tabs is really easy-going, and Dodie quite a gentle sort of person, so I knew neither of them would say anything.

"We were just wondering," said Tabs, "why you didn't learn about computers at your old school?"

Rachel giggled. I was beginning to notice that she always seemed to break into a giggle when she was embarrassed, or didn't want to answer a question.

"Didn't do it," she said. And, "Oops!" she added. "There's the bell. Mustn't be late!"

She shot off down the path, leaving the rest of us to follow at a more leisurely pace. It was only the first bell; there really wasn't any rush. A couple of Buttercups drew level with us – Dana, and her friend Maddy.

"Glad she's with you lot," said Dana.

Chantelle drew herself up. She looks very grand when she does that as she is tall to begin with. She said, "Meaning what, exactly?"

"Well…" Dana and Maddy both pulled faces. "Just glad you got saddled with her and not us!"

"What *is* their problem?" said Fawn, as the two of them walked off.

"They're idiots," said Tabs.

It was like, Rachel might be weird, but it was up to us to say so. We didn't need outsiders voicing their stupid opinions.

That evening in the dorm, before lights out, Rachel began on her nightly ritual with the rollers.

"What do you *do* that for?" demanded Fawn suddenly.

"I like to be curly," said Rachel.

"But you don't stay curly! It all comes out, and then it looks... well... kind of odd. Why can't you just leave it as it is?"

Rachel's face fell slightly.

"Honestly," said Fawn, "if you don't stop doing it, I'm not going to be able to walk around with you any more!"

"It makes people laugh," said Dodie. She said it quite kindly and gently, but Rachel's bottom lip was starting to quiver.

"You could just try leaving it for one night?" I said. "See what it looks like?"

"I know what it looks like. It looks horrible!"

We all stood around, gazing at Rachel's hair. It was long and wispy, with tons of split ends, all broken off at different lengths, like it hadn't been styled in ages. Maybe never.

"It just needs cutting," said Fawn.

"Cut it for me!"

"Me? I can't cut hair!"

"Why not wait till you get home and go to a proper hairdresser?" said Amy.

"No. Please! I want it done now." Rachel looked at me, imploringly. "Zoe?"

"No way," I said. "You'd end up bald."

"Somebody's got to! Dodie, you could do it."

"You wouldn't like it," said Dodie.

"I would, I would!"

"Well, it's not going to happen," said Fawn. "It's an art, cutting hair. You can't just pick up a pair of scissors and go at it."

"I can cut hair," said Chantelle.

We all turned to stare at her. Fawn said, "Really?" She sounded doubtful. Chantelle's hair is really short, clinging like a cap to her head. If she tried that with Rachel it would be a disaster. Rachel's hair would just lie limp and flat.

"Trust me," said Chantelle. "I'm good at it."

"Do it for me!" said Rachel.

"No, don't," said Fawn.

"Chantelle, *please!*" Rachel turned a tragic face towards Fawn. "I don't want people laughing."

We were all against it. I felt people would laugh even more if Chantelle got to work slashing and hacking. But Rachel begged so hard and Chantelle seemed so sure of herself that in the end even Fawn gave way.

"We'd better wait, it'll be lights out any minute. You don't want to rush it."

As soon as we felt safe, we switched on Rachel's bedside lamp and Chantelle set to work, using the scissors from Dodie's needlework kit. First she chopped, so that great lank wads of hair fell to the floor. (Fawn and I exchanged agonised glances.) Next she snipped – "Tidying up."

"Of course," she said, "these aren't really the right sort of scissors."

"I knew it!" said Fawn. "I knew we shouldn't let her!"

"I could do it far better if they were proper hairdressing ones."

"Or if you were a proper hairdresser," said Tabs.

"W-what's happening?" Rachel's voice quivered up at us as we stood round in the semi-darkness. "Is it all right?"

"It will be," said Chantelle. "Just let me shape it a bit."

More hair went floating to the floor. Fawn made a soft moaning sound.

"There you go." Chantelle stepped back, proudly. "Told you I could do it!"

She had too. She'd actually done it!

"Omigod," said Dodie, "that is so much better!"

"Let me see, let me see!"

"You'll have to go to the bathroom," said Chantelle, "if you want to have a proper look."

Rachel promptly went pattering off, down the hall. In wondering tones Fawn said, "You've made her look almost pretty."

It was true. Without the tattered curtain of hair hanging all round it her face was quite small and cheeky. And her eyes, I noticed almost for the first time, were grey-blue with really thick lashes.

"Whoever would have thought it?" said Tabs.

Rachel came back from the bathroom with one of her huge happy beams lighting up her face. She flung her arms round Chantelle's neck.

"Thank you, thank you, thank you!"

"At least now," said Tabs, "we won't be woken by loud *thumps* every morning."

She was referring to the seven o'clock ritual of Removing the Rollers, with Rachel still half asleep and

★ 79 ☆

her hand, exhausted, falling back every few seconds with a loud *flump* on the pillow.

"Relief all round," said Fawn.

"Yes," added Tabs, "and Dana and Maddy can stick *that* in their pipes and smoke it!"

"Stick what?" said Rachel, sounding puzzled.

"Their *attitude*," said Chantelle.

We went to bed very satisfied with ourselves.

Next morning, Rachel couldn't stop looking at herself. She was so excited! You'd have thought it was the first time in her life she'd ever had her hair cut.

"If you don't stop admiring yourself," said Fawn, in warning tones, "I shall have to take that mirror away from you."

Tabs added, "Yes, you'll go and break it if you're not careful. All that staring!"

"I can't help it," Rachel giggled. "I've never had my hair short before!"

"Big deal," said Chantelle. It seemed that for Rachel

it actually was. She couldn't wait to go down to breakfast and parade herself before everybody.

"Hey, Dana!" she said. She did a little twirl. "What do you think?"

If I'd been Rachel, Dana was the last person I'd have asked. I wouldn't even have wanted to *speak* to her, let alone invite her opinion; not the way she behaved. She was always making these mean little digs. But Rachel never seemed to bear grudges against anyone. She was always good-natured and obviously expected other people to be the same. A bit too trusting, if you asked me.

I waited for Dana to say something sour, like she usually did, but she must have been taken by surprise cos she just blinked and went, "I guess it's an improvement." Even that was grudging. I did wish Rachel wouldn't lay herself open! You really have to be a bit thick-skinned when you're dealing with people like Dana.

"I think Rachel looks lovely with her hair short," said Dodie.

"Yes, and I was the one that cut it," said Chantelle. She glared at Dana, like daring her to say something.

Dana just shrugged. "Whatever."

"Ignore her," said Fawn. "She's rubbish."

Rachel patted nervously at herself. "Does it really look all right?"

"Honestly," I assured her, as we took our places at the breakfast table, "you don't want to take any notice of Dana."

But the seeds of doubt had been sown. In one minute, Rachel had gone from being deliriously happy to totally downcast. It didn't take a lot to upset her. She was really, I was discovering, very insecure.

"Rachel, read my lips," said Fawn eventually. "IT'S LOOKING GOOD."

"Which it didn't before," I added, intending to be helpful but just managing to frighten her.

"Did I look really stupid?" she whispered.

"No! Of course you didn't. Just a bit... straggly. That's all."

"Now you look like a pixie," said Dodie. "A nice little pixie!"

Rachel beamed, gratefully.

"So if that's settled," said Fawn, "can we *please* move on to something else? I'm getting really bored with hair!"

In the end, we all got bored with it. Rachel just never knew when to stop. She was still fussing when we went home on Friday.

"I don't know what my auntie will say. Maybe she won't recognise me! Do I really look like a pixie? That could be my nickname… Pixie! What d'you think? Could I be Pixie?"

"It's not up to you," I said. "It's up to other people. That's what you told me! You said you couldn't choose your own nickname."

"Yes." She nodded, regretfully. "Other people have to do it for you."

None of the names she'd come up with had ever caught on. Thank goodness! I couldn't understand why she wanted one so badly. I was beginning to realise I couldn't really understand very much at all about Rachel; she was a complete mystery. It sometimes seemed like she was playing a part, trying to be like the girls she'd read about in old school stories. Like that was all she knew.

Still, at that moment I was feeling fond of her. After the hair-cutting episode, we'd all seemed to bond. She'd really enjoyed it when Fawn and Tabs had teased her about looking in the mirror. It was like for the first time she'd actually become one of us. I knew the others still thought she was weird, but I didn't get the feeling they thought I was weird for being friends with her. So when she suddenly said she'd had an idea, and wouldn't it be fun if we could do "one of those stay-over things", I didn't immediately panic and try to invent an excuse. I said, "Yes, it would! If you mean sleepover?"

"Sleepover." She nodded, happily. "I knew it was something like that! Shall I ask my auntie? See if you can come?"

I could have offered to invite *her*, cos I knew Mum wouldn't have any problems, but then there was Nat. If Nat was still going to be all prickly and suspicious, I wouldn't put it past her to make some of her stupid remarks, just cos Rachel was a bit different. I was starting to feel quite protective! I didn't want Rachel being hurt.

She called after me as I got off the train: "Shall I ask?"

I called back, "Yes! See you Sunday."

Nat was waiting on the platform with Dad. She immediately demanded to know what it was that Rachel was going to ask. Like it was any business of hers!

"What's it to you?" I said.

"I'm interested!"

"You mean you're *nosy*. It was a private conversation."

Nat pulled a face. So childish! After a bit she said, "She's had her hair cut. It looks better that way. It's still white, though."

"Blonde," I snapped.

Dad groaned. "Are we starting already?"

I firmly pressed my lips together and reminded myself what Mum had said, about Nat being scared in case I got all posh and above myself. I wouldn't, ever! But I could understand why it bothered her. St With's was as different as could be from our old school.

Mum was pleased when I told her about the hair-cutting session and how, as a result, we had all bonded.

"And now Rachel's going to ask if I can go for a sleepover at her place."

"Excellent!" said Mum. "Next time she can come here."

I was surprised, later that evening, when my phone rang and it was Rachel at the other end. I'd forgotten I'd given her my number. She was all bright and bubbly with excitement. Her auntie approved of her hair and Rachel had asked if we could have a sleepover and the answer was yes and how about next Friday?

"My auntie could pick us up after the theatre and you could come back with us!"

I said, "But I thought we'd decided to stay on at school?"

There was a bit of a pause, then Rachel said, "Oh."

"I mean… I thought we'd agreed," I said.

I hadn't meant to pour cold water over her plan, but I was so looking forward to being in school on Saturday morning. I could almost *hear* Rachel's face dropping. She was so easily upset. In spite of all her giggles and her bounciness, she was really quite unsure of herself. So then, of course, I felt bad, like I'd snubbed her or something.

"We could always do it the week after," I said.

A long quivering sigh came down the telephone. "Only if you really want to."

"I do!" I said. "It's just that – you know! This Friday? Mum's already put in a request."

"Request for what?" said Mum, as I rang off.

"Extra night's boarding," I said. "Cos of the theatre trip. Rachel wanted me to go back with her for a sleepover."

"Well, you could," said Mum. "We can always cancel the boarding. I'm sure they won't mind."

But I didn't want to!

"It's all right," I said. "We can do it the following week."

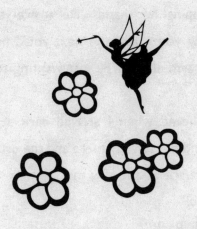

CHAPTER FIVE

It was silly, but I actually spent a lot of the weekend worrying that I might have destroyed Rachel's confidence. She seemed to have so little! But really I hadn't done anything wrong so I don't know why I should have felt guilty. Rachel got you like that. One minute you'd be wanting to scream at her – like when she carried on and on about something, or skipped around clapping her hands like a five-year-old and embarrassing you – and the next you'd find yourself feeling all warm and slurpy, just wanting to take care of her.

I was relieved when I arrived back at school on Sunday to find her already there and the usual big beam splitting her face as she saw me.

"Zoeeeee!"

I said, "Hi, Rach."

She started burbling straight away. "I asked her! My auntie. I asked her about the stay-over. She said it'd be OK to do it the following week cos that's when it's half term. She said to see if it's OK for you. Is it OK?" She looked at me, anxiously. "You could still come on the Friday and my auntie could take you back to the station next day. So is that all right, do you think?"

I said, "I'm sure it will be. I'll just have to check with Mum in case she's made any plans, but I don't think she has."

"Check with her now," begged Rachel. "Please, Zoe, please! Do it now!"

I knew if I didn't give in she would just keep nagging. She stood by me, gnawing at a fingernail, as I made the call. The others all hung around, pretending not to listen and listening just as hard as they could.

"It's OK," I reported. "Half term is fine."

"Thank God for that," said Fawn. "The suspense was killing me."

"Yay!" Rachel did one of her little skippity-hops round the dorm.

Fawn shook her head, Chantelle rolled her eyes, Tabs giggled. I just cringed. It was one of those moments. Why did she always, *always* have to go and ruin everything? It was so embarrassing! Little did I know, there was more to come...

Friday was the day we were going to the theatre. Rachel was so excited! All week long she'd kept telling us how she'd been shopping with her auntie and they'd bought her this new dress, specially.

"*Specially?*" said Fawn.

"Yes!" Rachel bounced, happily. "A new dress, specially!"

"Just for going to the theatre?"

"It's an occasion," said Rachel, all self-important, like it was something Fawn should know without having to be told. "But I'm not letting you see it till the last moment!"

"Can't wait," said Fawn.

"You do realise," added Chantelle, "that we're not going to meet the Queen?"

Rachel giggled. She obviously thought Chantelle was being funny.

Friday after tea, we went up to the dorm to change. That was when we finally got to see it. The Dress. Omigod, I nearly died! It was bright yellow and all hung about with *bits*. Bobbly bits. Silly little puffy sleeves and a big bell skirt. And Rachel inside it, simpering and twirling, inviting my approval.

"What d'you think?"

"I –" I swallowed – "It's... um – uh…"

Horrible was the word that immediately sprang to my lips. Fortunately the others arrived before I could actually say it. Fawn gave a shriek.

"Is that it?"

"It's her dress," I said.

"That's what you're wearing?"

They all stood, transfixed. Rachel stopped her twirling and put a finger in her mouth.

"Her new dress." I pulled back my lips, sending an agonised grimace in Fawn's direction. "*Her new dress that her auntie bought her. Specially.*"

Fawn got the message. "Very eye-catching," she said.

"D'you like it?" said Rachel.

"Wouldn't suit everybody," said Tabs.

"Wouldn't suit *anybody*," snorted Chantelle, when Rachel had gone off to the bathroom.

"Hasn't she got anything else?"

They all turned, accusingly, to me, as if I could do anything about it.

"It's grotesque," moaned Fawn. "And *yellow*. Yuck!"

I had to agree. Even apart from the general awfulness of it, yellow was just about the worst colour she could have chosen. It made her look all washed out, like she had some sort of ghastly disease.

"You're her friend," said Chantelle, poking at me. "Tell her!"

But how could I? She was so proud of herself!

"It's going to make people laugh at her," warned Tabs.

"It's going to make people laugh at *us*," said Fawn. "Unless we disown her?"

"I think we should," urged Chantelle.

Even Chantelle and Tabs were agreeing they would rather not be seen in the company of such horror.

"I vote we tell her," said Fawn. "Either she puts on something else or we don't want to know."

They were looking at me again. I turned, rather helplessly, to Dodie. "What do you think?"

"It wouldn't be very kind," said Dodie.

"Not very kind if people laugh at her, either," said Fawn.

"Well, no, but they wouldn't do it to her face. It's not like she'd actually *know*."

"We will!"

"Oh!" Chantelle tossed her head. "What's it matter? Let her wear it, if it makes her happy. She's totally bonkers and that's all there is to it. At least we've got her hair sorted. We can work on her wardrobe later."

I was so grateful to Chantelle. And to Dodie. Fawn was obviously running out of patience. She is one of those people that just hates to look ridiculous. Well, I don't suppose anybody actually *likes* looking ridiculous, but it is worse for someone like Fawn. She is so slim and pretty, and always so elegant. I could see that being seen with some weird bonkers person in a vile yellow dress all hung about with bobbles would be seriously upsetting for her image.

Still, the rest of us had fun getting ready together. It was just as I'd imagined boarding school would be! Even Fawn seemed to forget her mood for a while as we compared outfits. She herself was wearing this beautiful daisy-print skirt, while the rest of us were all in skinny jeans and sparkly tops. Rachel's eyes widened as she saw us. She said, "Oh! *Jeans*. I didn't know we could wear jeans!" I thought of suggesting she quickly go and change into a pair, but the only ones I'd ever seen on her were a bit baggy and shapeless, and besides she had bought the yellow dress specially. It would have seemed a shame not to let her wear it when she was so proud and happy. And the others, by now, all seemed resigned.

We mostly kept our coats on in the school bus that took us to Norwich so it wasn't till we reached the theatre that Rachel was displayed in all her glory. I expect one or two people did snigger quietly to themselves, but if they did I didn't notice, and thank goodness Rachel didn't, either. Dana came up to us in the interval and said, "And what has she come as? A daffodil?"

To which Chantelle smartly retorted, "Or is she a Buttercup?"

"No way!" said Dana.

"No way!" giggled Rachel. "Who'd want to be a Buttercup?"

"Nobody with any sense," said Tabs.

I didn't think Fawn had heard. She had been doing her best to distance herself, going over to join some Days, chatting in a corner. Rachel had already embarrassed her – and me, to be honest – by laughing far too long and far too loudly whenever anything funny had happened in the play, and by refusing to stop clapping when the curtain came down. I'd had to jog her elbow, in the end, and say, "That's enough, Rach!" so I wasn't really surprised when Fawn went stalking off.

Still, something must have got through to her, because at the end of the evening, as we boarded the bus to take us back to St With's, she gave Rachel a little nudge and said, "Go on, Daffy! Get in."

Rachel scurried after me. We always sat together. In tones of pure delight she hissed, "*Daffy!*" She was pleased as could be.

On Monday in English, Miss Seymour said that now we had actually seen the play she had an end-of-term project for us. She wanted us to divide into three groups – Daisies, Buttercups and day girls – and for each to put on a short scene, no longer than ten minutes, using Shakespeare's characters.

Dana said, "*Any* of Shakespeare's characters?"

"Any from *A Midsummer Night's Dream*," said Miss Seymour.

"Ah. Right." Dana turned and nodded self-importantly at the rest of us. "Any from *A Midsummer Night's Dream*. And no longer than ten minutes."

Us Daisies stared at her, pityingly. Who did she think she was impressing? She was truly pathetic! Even Rachel at her embarrassing worst wasn't as bad as Dana and her know-it-all bossiness.

I was going through another one of my being-fond-of-Rachel phases. On the train going home on Saturday she'd babbled nonstop about having a nickname at last.

"And all because of my dress! Wait till I tell my auntie... *She* didn't want me to buy it."

I wondered, in that case, why she had let her. Still, at least Rachel had got the nickname that she'd so badly wanted. She wasn't to know that Fawn had tried to disown her.

Miss Seymour told us that we would all get to perform our Shakespeare scenes on stage, in front of the whole school.

"So I'd like you to go away and think about it," she said, "and see what you can come up with."

At break next day Fawn gathered us all together and announced that she had had an idea.

"We could do our own version of the scene where

Titania wakes up and sees Bottom wearing the ass's head and falls in love with him."

She looked at us, expectantly. Waiting, no doubt, for someone to go, "Yesss!"

"Where would we get an ass's head?" wondered Tabs.

"We'd make it! No problem. It would be really funny," urged Fawn. "And there's just the right number of parts: Titania, Bottom and four fairies."

"Fairies," said Chantelle. She pulled a face.

Hurriedly, Fawn said, "There don't necessarily *have* to be four of them. There don't have to be any at all, if we don't want them. It's just that I've thought of something really funny for them to do!"

"But they're *not* funny," said Dodie. "Not in Shakespeare."

"We can make them funny! We don't have to use Shakespeare's words."

"So whose words are we going to use?"

"Ours!" said Fawn.

"*Ours?*" Tabs sounded alarmed. "Why can't we just use Shakespeare's?"

"Cos his fairies aren't any fun. Mine are going to be *fun*," said Fawn.

Doubtfully, Tabs said, "Oh."

"Look, just don't worry! I'll see to it. I've got it all worked out."

"I'm not going to be a fairy," said Chantelle.

Fawn heaved a sigh.

"All right, you can be… something else. Oberon! I'll bring Oberon into it. You're too tall for a fairy, anyway. Though on the other hand a really *tall* fairy—"

"No." Chantelle put on her stubborn expression. When she decides she doesn't want to do something, there is no moving her. "I don't mind being Oberon, but I'm not going to be a fairy.

"OK, OK," said Fawn. "You be Oberon."

"Right." Chantelle nodded. She liked that idea.

Tabs, rather nervously, said, "What about Bottom? Who's going to play him?"

"I thought Zoe."

"Oh! Yes." The relief in Tabs's voice was obvious. In all honesty, she is a bit plump for playing fairies, but on the other hand, who would want to play Bottom? All rude and crude and wearing an ass's head?

"Zoe," said Tabs, in tones of deep satisfaction. "She'd be great!"

I would? "Why me?" I said.

"Cos when you read it in class the other day, you had us all in fits," said Fawn.

It was true, I'd got everyone laughing. I'd used what Dad calls a 'hayseed' accent, which is really just a sort of pretend West Country and which I can only do cos of one of my grans coming from there. We are always teasing her when she says 'oi' instead of 'I'. But I had played it up a bit! Miss Seymour had said, "That was shameless, Zoe! But you certainly breathed a bit of life into the part."

"Everyone else," said Fawn, "was just so wooden." She meant everyone else except her. Fawn really fancies herself as an actor. To be fair to her, she is actually good. Well, *very* good, in all honesty. "Being able to make people laugh," she said, "is a real gift."

I couldn't help feeling flattered. Fawn doesn't very often praise anyone; she is quite a critical sort of person.

"OK," I said. Maybe I wouldn't mind playing Bottom. He was one of the main parts, after all.

"And don't worry," Fawn promised, "I'll give the fairies lots of proper words to say."

"Can I be Peaseblossom?" begged Dodie.

"Yes! You can be Peaseblossom, Tabs can be Mustard Seed and Daffy can be Cobweb. Cos of your hair," Fawn explained. "All nice and cobwebby."

"Well," I said to Rachel, as we wandered back into school, "that should be fun! Don't you think?"

Rachel bit her lip and didn't say anything. She didn't even giggle.

"When Fawn said about your hair being cobwebby, she didn't mean anything bad," I assured her. "She just meant it's, like… very fine and delicate. Like cobwebs. It was a compliment, if anything."

Still Rachel said nothing. So then I thought perhaps she was upset because of not being given one of the leads.

"It is going to be a proper part," I reminded her. "Not like in the play where you just say stuff like 'Hail!' and 'Cobweb!' You're going to have real lines. And maybe," I added, on a note of sudden inspiration, "if you asked Fawn to let you play Mustard Seed instead of Cobweb, you could wear your dress! Nice yellow daffodil dress."

After all, Fawn had said the fairies were going to be funny. What could be funnier than a bright yellow dress all covered in bobbles?

"Honestly, it'll be fun," I said. "On stage, like in a real theatre. In front of the whole school. I'm looking forward to it!"

I was wittering, now. Just blabbering on, trying to get some sort of response out of her. But I couldn't. And then, a few days later, she dropped her bombshell.

CHAPTER SIX

"You can't do it?" Fawn's voice rose in disbelief. "What do you mean, you can't do it?"

"I can't do it," said Rachel.

"Why can't you?"

"Cos I can't."

She said it apologetically, like she knew she was

letting people down, and especially Fawn, who had gone to such trouble writing pages and pages of script, but still she *said* it. Over and over. It was all we could get out of her: she couldn't do it. She wouldn't even say why. When pushed, she just said that she didn't want to. Didn't want to, wasn't going to. And that was that.

I would never have guessed she could be so stubborn. She was worse than Chantelle. At least with Chantelle you could understand *why* she didn't want to do things. Like not wanting to be a fairy. Chantelle was the under-fifteens hockey captain. Hockey captains don't get all dressed up in little flimsy dresses with gauzy wings attached. She didn't need to explain. But Rachel did, and she just wouldn't! It made us all lose patience with her. Even me.

Dodie, trying to be helpful, said that if she was scared of stage fright, she wouldn't be alone.

"I was absolutely *paralysed* last year, when we did *The Snow Queen*! I was, wasn't I?" She turned to the others for confirmation. They all solemnly nodded. "I was, like, all shaky and trembling and feeling sick."

"That's right," agreed Fawn. "You kept wailing that you couldn't go on."

"Yes, cos I couldn't remember any of my lines!"

Dodie looked expectantly at Rachel. We all looked at Rachel. Rachel just munched on her lip and said nothing. What was the *matter* with her?

"I couldn't even remember the first few words," said Dodie. "I just wanted to run away and hide!"

"So what happened?" I said.

"Oh. Well! Everybody told me I'd be all right once I was on stage, and someone gave me this huge shove—"

"That was me," said Chantelle.

"*Was* it? I never knew that before!"

"It worked, though, didn't it? It got you on stage."

"*And* saying your lines," prompted Fawn.

"Yes! They all came back to me. Just like that! They do," said Dodie. "Honestly!"

"It's not as if you've got that many, anyway," said Fawn. She was beginning to sound quite irritated. "There's only about six of them! It's not very much to ask, I wouldn't have thought."

"It's not," I agreed, feeling that I had to speak up in support. Fawn had worked so hard on her script! And she had taken real care to give everyone a proper part. She had explained to us that every single line was important.

"I can't just give yours to someone else," she told Rachel. "It would throw everything out!"

"In any case," said Tabs, "we're all supposed to take part."

"This is it," said Chantelle. "We're a *team*."

Rachel took a deep breath, like she had come to some big decision. We waited, hopefully.

"I wouldn't mind helping backstage," she said.

Fawn made an impatient scoffing sound. "We don't *need* any help backstage! It's not like it's some big production. We're not having loads of props or scenery."

"No, but I could help with the costumes and stuff. Like for Bottom! When he wakes up wearing a donkey's head. I can think of ways we could do it! I'd be good at that!"

"It's an ass's head, *actually*," said Fawn.

To be honest I am not at all sure what the difference is, but I had been wondering myself how we would manage it. Fawn, however, dismissed the idea somewhat crushingly.

"It's not going to be a complete head, and I know exactly how we're going to do it, thank you very much. We just need you to play your part, same as everyone else."

"It really doesn't matter if you can't act," said Dodie, anxious as ever to reassure. "I can't act, either! Fawn's the only one that really can."

I thought, *Well, and me, maybe*. After all, I had made them laugh.

"You just have to say the lines," said Tabs. "That's all."

We might as well have saved our breath. The

more we tried to reason with her, the more she refused to budge. She just stood, like a block of cement. In the end she became so sullen that we just gave up.

Everybody was so angry with her! I really couldn't blame them.

"Honestly," said Fawn, "she is such a pain! I've written her a really nice little part, a *really* nice little part. I don't know why I bothered!"

Chantelle turned to me. "Can't *you* say something?"

I said, "Like what?"

"I don't know! Think of something!"

They were all doing that thing they did, that laser thing with their eyes. All boring into me. *You're her friend! You think of something!*

Not for the first time, I found myself almost wishing that I hadn't got tied up with Rachel in the first place. This was a thousand times worse than just being embarrassed by her! It was turning all the others against me.

Rather tearfully, I rang Mum and told her that I didn't want to sleep over at Rachel's that weekend after all. Mum naturally wanted to know why, so I told her, thinking she would take my side and agree that Rachel was behaving selfishly and being totally disloyal. Instead, she seemed to think that *I* was the one being disloyal.

"I thought Rachel was your friend?" she said. "Friends are meant to stand by each other."

"But, Mum," I cried, "she's letting people down!" And not just the others. She was letting *me* down, as well. Friends weren't supposed to do that.

"Well, I don't think it would be very kind if you backed out at this stage," said Mum. "Not when she's so excited about it. That's what you told me!"

It was true: Rachel *was* excited. And I had been quite looking forward to seeing where she lived and meeting her auntie and the gran she sometimes mentioned. But that was before she'd gone and upset everyone! And now they were all turning on me like it was my fault. Like I was responsible for her behaviour.

"It's only the one night…" urged Mum. "I really think you should go. After all, you did promise."

I pouted into the phone. "Oh, all right," I said. "If I must."

"Don't be like that," said Mum. "You were happy enough at the beginning to have Rachel as a friend."

I thought again, rather vengefully, that none of this would ever have happened if Nat hadn't gone and got the chicken pox and breathed it over me. I'd already have made friends with Fawn and the others before Rachel even arrived on the scene.

Rachel herself was obviously feeling anxious. She asked me, on Thursday evening, if we were still having our stay-over.

"Sleepover!" I snapped.

In almost frightened tones, like she'd committed some sort of crime, she said, "Sorry! Sleepover. You are still going to come?"

I was aware of the others standing nearby, their ears flapping. I muttered, "Yes, of course I am."

Her face immediately lit up with one of her big goofy smiles. "Oh, goody!" she said. (I winced. *Oh, goody?*) "My auntie's going to pick us up. She's ever so looking forward to meeting you."

"Me too," I mumbled.

The others had their own plans for half term. Dodie was flying out to Hong Kong to be with her mum and dad; Tabs was going to stay with her sister, who lived on the Isle of Wight; Chantelle was spending the week with Fawn.

"Have fun," said Fawn, as we all prepared to go our separate ways on Friday.

"Just see if you can *do* something," hissed Chantelle.

She meant, do something to make Rachel change her mind. I promised that I would try, though to be honest I really didn't want to. Rachel would only clam up again and I would get impatient and I just had this feeling that it wouldn't do the slightest bit of good.

Still, I'd promised Chantelle that I would give it a go. Sitting on the train, with Rachel sitting opposite, I dutifully racked my brains trying to think of some way I could bring the subject up, but nothing came. We just sat there in silence, me staring out of the window and Rachel reading a magazine. It was most unlike Rachel not to be chattering practically nonstop and actually I think she was only pretending to read cos quite suddenly she leaned forward and said, "You know *why* Fawn's so desperate to do this scene, don't you?"

I said, "Yes, she wants to beat the Buttercups!" It wasn't supposed to be a competition, but I'd discovered there was a strong rivalry between the two dorms. Not so much between the Days. "She wants ours to be the best!"

"It's not just that," Rachel said, scornfully. "It's cos she wants to play Titania and get all dressed up and look pretty so everyone will go on about how wonderful she is."

I was quite shocked when Rachel said that. I couldn't think how to respond. I had never, ever known Rachel to be vindictive. It just wasn't her.

"As for making you play that horrible ugly Bottom," she said, "that's really mean!"

"Bottom's not horrible," I protested. "He's funny! It's a good part."

"It'll make you look stupid," said Rachel. "Why can't she play it herself, if it's so good?"

"Well, cos she's more suited to Titania," I said.

"Huh!" Rachel snorted.

"Anyway," I added, "she's not *making* me play Bottom. I can always say if I don't want to."

"Ho, yes!" Rachel made a scoffing sound. "You just try it!"

I frowned. I was starting to feel quite uncomfortable. Something was going on here. Something I didn't understand. Rachel had been so thrilled about going to the theatre, almost like it was the first time she'd ever been. She'd talked about it for days before and for days afterwards, until, as usual, we'd all got sick of hearing about it. Now, just the idea of playing a tiny little part in a tiny little scene and she was acting like we wanted her to do something disgusting. It was *Shakespeare*! You couldn't get much more proper than Shakespeare.

"Would *you* have liked to play Titania?" I said.

"I don't want to play anything," said Rachel.

"But why not?"

"Cos I don't!"

Again, it was all she would say. As a rule, when she didn't want to talk about things, she burst into peals of giggles. Not this time; it was like she was feeling threatened in some way. I decided that I would have to let the subject drop or the weekend would be unbearable. I'd done my best; I couldn't do any more.

I went back to staring out of the window. Rachel went back to her magazine. I slid my eyes sideways. It was a fashion magazine. Rachel wasn't into fashion!

Unless, perhaps, she was trying to learn? I watched her for a while. She was just flicking through the pages. Right through to the end, then back again to the beginning. The silence began to feel uncomfortable.

"What sort of car does your auntie drive?" I said.

"A red one," said Rachel.

She said it quite solemnly; she wasn't being funny. *A red one*. I could have said, *No, I meant what make?*, but I wasn't really interested in the make. I'd just been trying to get some kind of conversation going.

"My dad's got a new car," I said. "We never had one before. Just a van."

"My auntie's never had one before," said Rachel. "She only passed her test a few months ago."

Well, at least we were talking again. Not about anything very inspiring, but it was better than just sitting saying nothing.

By the time we pulled into Rachel's station, we were back to normal. I'd moved over to sit next to her and we were going through her magazine together, commenting on the models and what they were wearing.

"That's pretty," said Rachel, pointing to something utterly hideous. Skin-tight trousers, bright green with yellow stripes like a snake. Yuck!

"You'd have to have the figure for it," I said.

"Like Fawn," agreed Rachel. "She could wear just about anything."

We both sighed.

"She is so lucky," said Rachel.

She didn't sound like she was jealous. Just a bit envious. But I was a bit envious too, so that was all right.

"Look, there's my auntie," said Rachel, as we left the train.

She pointed to someone waiting at the barrier. A big bony person, wearing thick tweedy sort of clothes and clumpy shoes. Definitely not a fashion icon! But she had a large friendly face, which broke into a beam just like Rachel's, which made me feel immediately that I was going to like her.

She said, "Hello! Are you Zoe? I'm so glad you could come – we're very excited about it. I'm Auntie Helen, by the way."

She stuck out her hand, so I stuck mine out, and she laughed and pumped it up and down.

"Oh, you're going to have fun," she said. "Rachel's arranged a real spread… all her favourite foods! Very naughty, but once in a while doesn't hurt. Just don't go telling your mum!"

She winked as she said it, and Rachel giggled, so I did too. It was all a bit odd, and not what I was expecting, but it's nice when you go somewhere and you're made to feel welcome. I'd once visited a friend from primary school and been totally miserable the whole time, cos her mum had made it plain as could be that she didn't really want me there. Rachel's auntie Helen made it seem like I was doing them some sort of favour, like I was royalty, or something.

I don't quite know what sort of place I'd imagined Rachel living in. A gingerbread cottage, maybe. Certainly something different. I was quite surprised when the car pulled up outside a perfectly ordinary block of flats.

"I'll just see you both inside," said Auntie Helen.

I was puzzled. What did she mean? She wasn't going to stay?

"Oh, I don't live here," she told me. "It's just Rachel and her gran. I have a place of my own."

It wasn't terribly cheerful inside the flat. Dark, and poky, and a bit dingy. Rachel's gran was sitting in an armchair with a rug over her legs. She looked quite stern and forbidding. Old too. Far older than either of my grans. She was dressed all in black, with her hair scraped back into some kind of bun. I couldn't decide if it was white or just very blonde, like Rachel's. White, I think.

Auntie Helen said, "Auntie, this is Zoe. Rachel's friend. Zoe, this is Rachel's gran."

The old lady just nodded. She didn't even say hallo. She didn't even smile. She hardly even moved her head. I felt my heart sink. Rachel's gran obviously didn't want me here. I knew I shouldn't have come!

CHAPTER SEVEN

"I'll settle the girls," said Auntie Helen, "and then I'll be off."

Still the old lady didn't say anything. Just sat there, looking grim. Auntie Helen said, "Auntie? Is that all right?"

The old lady shrugged a shoulder.

"Come on, then, girls! Let's go and sort out what you're eating."

We followed Auntie Helen down the hall to a poky little kitchen.

"Here we are," said Auntie Helen, handing us a couple of Tupperware containers. "I got it all ready for you. Enjoy! What time do you think you'll want to go home tomorrow, Zoe?"

I felt like saying, *I'd like to go home right now!* But of course I couldn't. I mumbled, "After breakfast, maybe?"

"As early as that?" Auntie Helen seemed surprised.

Ever so quickly I said, "Mum wants me back. We're going somewhere."

"Oh! All right, no problem. I'll be round about ten o'clock to pick you up. Is that OK?"

I nodded. There wasn't much else I could do.

"See you both tomorrow, then. Have fun!"

I so didn't want Auntie Helen to leave! I felt like I was being abandoned in some kind of witch's den with a big black spider lurking in the corner, waiting to pounce. I am not the sort of person to be scared of things. Like, I have never been scared of the dark, for instance, or even of spiders if it comes to that, but the atmosphere in this place was definitely spooky. I'd noticed that since we'd arrived even Rachel had been strangely subdued. Not at all her normal bubbly self.

We stood in the doorway, clutching our Tupperware containers. Rachel said, "We're going to go and eat our tea now, Gran."

The old lady inclined her head and made a grunting sound. I was struck by a sudden guilty thought: maybe she'd had a stroke or something? Maybe that was why she just sat there looking disagreeable and not saying anything?

"We'll probably stay in my room," said Rachel.

The old lady waved a hand, like, *Suit yourself.*

Rachel led the way back down the narrow hall and threw open a door with a flourish.

"This is my room!" She sounded like she was really proud of it. It was how I'd felt when I'd finally got a room of my own in our new big house and didn't have to share with Nat any more.

Rachel's room was cramped, the same as the rest of the flat, but unlike the rest of the flat it wasn't dingy and dark. There were bright yellow curtains and a bright yellow duvet cover with a pattern of red flowers. Rachel obviously had a thing about yellow. It is not a colour I really go for, but at least it cheered the place up. Like the pictures pinned to the walls and all the ornaments scattered about. The pictures looked like they had come from calendars. Flowers and birds and cherry trees. Not a pop star in sight! The ornaments seemed mostly to be animals – like, there was a donkey wearing a straw hat and a bear standing on its hind legs beating a drum – but there was also an old-fashioned lady wearing a crinoline and one that looked like a shepherdess. The sort of thing my gran has.

It was all a bit odd and not at all like my bedroom, but it was friendly and cosy, so I immediately began to feel a bit happier. Rachel did too; I could tell. She was suddenly back to the Rachel who sometimes drove me mad but who I realised, again, I was actually quite fond of. With all her giggles and her weird behaviour, she was too good-natured for anyone to stay cross with for long. (Though I still thought she was being selfish and unreasonable, refusing to take part in Fawn's Shakespeare's scene. It was hard to forgive her for that.)

"Let's see what we've got," she said, sitting cross-legged on the floor with her Tupperware box.

"I thought you knew?" I said. I sank down beside her. Her room was so tiny there was only just space for the two of us. "I thought you were the one that chose it all?"

"I told Auntie Helen what to get, and – yes!" She'd peeled back the lid of her container. Triumphantly, she showed me the contents. "All my favourite goodies! What's in yours? See if it's the same!"

Obediently I peeled back my own lid. My eyes did this boggling thing, like staring so hard they nearly fell out of their sockets. I said, "Blimey!" Blimey is one of my dad's favourite expressions. I don't use it very often, but just sometimes it's the only word I can think of.

"What, what?" said Rachel. "Let's see!"

I held out the container. It was like a dozen Christmases all rolled into one. Crunchie bars and Mars bars, crisps and Pringles and sausage rolls, big puffy marshmallows, Chocolate Oranges, little cakes with bright pink icing.

"Is it all right?" said Rachel. "Is it the sort of thing you like?"

I said, "It's the sort of thing my mum would go demented about."

Rachel's face fell. "Would she be angry?"

"She wouldn't be *angry*. She'd be like, *Omigod, Zoe, all that sugar!* How about your gran? Doesn't she mind?"

Rachel shook her head. "Gran doesn't know. Auntie Helen kept it a secret. Like when we went to the theatre? That was a secret as well."

I was puzzled. "You mean your gran wouldn't have wanted you to go?"

"She wouldn't have let me. She's very strict. So whatever you do," said Rachel, earnestly, "you mustn't mention it to her."

I promised that I wouldn't, though it didn't really seem to me at all likely that I would ever be given the opportunity to do so. The horrid old woman obviously didn't want to talk to me.

"She doesn't say very much," I said, "does she? Your gran."

"Not since my granddad died," said Rachel.

That immediately made me start feeling guilty again, like when I thought maybe she'd had a stroke.

"Did she love him a lot?" I said. I was thinking of one of my own grans, who had been what Mum called *inconsolable* when Granddad had died.

"Not really," said Rachel. "I don't think anybody did, really."

I didn't know what to say to that. I reached out for a sausage roll.

"Auntie Helen says he wasn't a very loveable sort

of person," said Rachel. "She says that Gran isn't, either, but it's not her fault. She's been crushed."

I frowned, and nibbled on my roll. This was turning into a very odd conversation.

"Why did Auntie Helen call your gran 'auntie'?" I said. I wasn't that interested. It was just something to break the silence.

"Cos that's what she is," said Rachel. "Auntie Helen's dad was Granddad's brother. Auntie Helen's been crushed as well, but she's getting over it. She doesn't think that Gran ever will. Not now. She's been crushed for too long, and anyway she's too old. You won't ever tell anyone, will you?"

"Um – n-no," I said. "Not if you don't want me to."

"People wouldn't understand," said Rachel.

I wasn't sure that I did. But in any case, who would I tell? Maybe Fawn and the others. They would be interested to know what it was like, having a sleepover with Rachel. But if she'd rather I didn't, then I wouldn't.

"I'm only telling you," said Rachel, "cos you're my friend."

I nodded. "Right." I couldn't help wondering where her dad was, but I didn't quite like to ask. I wouldn't have wanted to upset her. Mum is always telling me not to be pushy.

"Hey!" Rachel suddenly leaned forward and plunged a hand under the bed. "Look what I've got us for later!"

"Oh, *yuck*," I said. "You can't be serious?"

She'd pulled out a can of sardines and a tin of condensed milk. Plus a tin opener. She *was* serious. She actually expected me to eat sardines dunked in condensed milk!

"It'll be our own private midnight feast." She beamed at me. "Even Auntie Helen doesn't know about it! I've got something else as well." She slid her hand back under the bed and scrabbled round for a bit. "See?"

She was waving something at me. I said, "Playing cards?"

She nodded, blissfully. "I found them. I thought you could teach me that game you were telling me about."

I said, "What game?" I was at a loss. I couldn't remember telling her about any game.

"When we first met, and I said I'd had chicken pox and you said 'snap'."

"Oh. Yes!" It all came back to me. "It's not really a grown-up game," I said. "It's for little kids." And then, hurriedly, in case she thought I was putting her down: "We could play it, if you really want."

"I want to learn," insisted Rachel.

"There isn't much to it," I said. "All you do, you just share out the cards so we each have a pile, then we turn them over one at a time, and if two cards are the same, like two sixes or two jacks or something, the first to shout 'Snap!' picks up all the cards in the pile and the winner is the person that ends up with the whole lot. Dead easy! I'll show you." I dealt out the cards. "D'you want to go first?"

Rachel said, "OK." She seemed doubtful. Why was she crinkling her forehead like that? What didn't she understand?

"What's a jack?" she said.

Omigod! Didn't she know anything? Patiently I gathered all the cards up again and showed her the jacks, and the kings and the queens. "And these are aces," I said. Rachel shook her head, wonderingly. I could see that it was all just completely new to her. Like computers. Whoever heard of anybody not even knowing how to switch a computer on? It was like she'd been brought up in a different century. Still, she was really eager to learn. She laughed when she finally got the idea of how to play Snap.

"This is fun!" she said. "I've got another game here!" She dived back under the bed. "Snakes and Ladders! D'you know that one?"

I didn't tell her that Snakes and Ladders was also a game for little kids. She was so happy that she'd learnt to play Snap!

"I put stuff under here," she said, "so Gran can't find it. Her knees are bad. She can't get down here."

Wonderingly I said, "What would she do if she could?"

"If she found them?" Rachel's eyes went big. "She'd be shocked!"

I wanted to ask why. *Why* would she be shocked? What was shocking about Snakes and Ladders? But I was scared that Rachel would suddenly clam up, like she so often did when I got too curious. At least she had *started* to talk, even if I couldn't make much sense of it. It would probably be best if I didn't push her. Mum would be proud of me! She is always saying that I am like a bull in a china shop, just trampling all over everything without bothering to think.

"What's this?" I said, tugging at a cardboard box that was sticking out from under the bed.

"Oh!" Rachel immediately snatched it. "Those are my photographs. I found them in one of those bin things. Things people throw stuff away in."

"A skip," I said.

"Yes. Someone was clearing out an office. It wasn't stealing! They were just being chucked out. I find lots of things that way. You'd be amazed what people get rid of! Like all my ornaments."

I turned to look at them. I could see, now, that most were damaged in some way. The donkey with the straw hat had an ear missing and the bear standing on its hind legs had a chip in its side.

Defensively, Rachel said, "There isn't any reason to throw things away just cos they're not new any more."

"I suppose not," I said.

"Gran doesn't believe in spending money on fribbles. That's what she calls them. She doesn't really approve of ornaments at all, but this is my room and Auntie Helen says I can have fribbles if I want. Shall we play Snakes and Ladders?"

I said, "Oh! Yes. OK." I was still wondering what sort of person didn't approve of ornaments.

"I've been reading what it says on the box," said

Rachel. "I think I understand the rules... You go *down* the snakes and *up* the ladders. Is that right?"

I agreed that it was. "But we need dice. Are there some dice in there?"

"You mean these little things?"

I said, "Ye-e-e-s."

This really was the oddest sleepover I'd ever been to! I mean, who plays Snap and Snakes and Ladders when they're thirteen years old? Actually, to my surprise – though I would never have admitted it to someone like Fawn, who can be *so* superior – I found that I was quite enjoying it. Rachel grew all fizzy with excitement, whizzing down snakes at breakneck speed and shouting "Yay!" every time she shot up a ladder. Her enthusiasm was catching. Before I knew it, I was also whizzing down snakes and crying "Yay!" as I shot up ladders. I didn't dare to think what Nat would have to say about it. She was someone else I wouldn't tell!

At eleven o'clock, Rachel declared, very solemnly, that now we had to drink cocoa.

"Why's that?" I said.

"Cos it's what you do. It's all part of it."

Together we crept along the dark passage to the kitchen. Rachel put her finger to her lips and said, "Sh! Careful not to wake Gran."

"Which is her room?" I whispered.

"That one." Rachel pointed. "But it's all right, she's a bit deaf."

The kitchen was really horrible. Even dingier than the one we'd had in our old flat, before Mum and Dad won the lottery. Mum had always complained that the kitchen was like a cupboard. This one was more like a coffin. It was creepy! I was glad when we'd made the cocoa and could go back to Rachel's room.

As we sat sipping our cocoa, Rachel suddenly said, "Do you have a boyfriend?"

I swallowed a mouthful of cocoa far too hot, and spluttered, "Boyfriend?" It was just so unexpected, coming from Rachel.

"I know they don't in Enid Blyton," said Rachel, "but

Auntie Helen says things have changed since then. Like, these days most people our age would have boyfriends, right?"

"Not necessarily," I said. "I mean, some people do. Not everyone."

"Have you?" said Rachel.

I said, "Me?" I only repeated it to give myself a bit of time, deciding how to answer. "There was this boy at my old school I quite fancied. John Arthur. We went out for a bit."

"What happened? Did you break up?"

I said, "No, we moved and things just sort of fizzled out. And then I came to St With's."

Rachel nodded, understandingly. "No boys. Would you rather be at a school with boys?"

"Dunno." I frowned, as I thought about it. "Sometimes I think I would. But then it kind of puts pressure on you."

"Mm." Rachel considered it a moment. "I bet Fawn's got a boyfriend," she said.

I said, "Oh, well, Fawn." She was the sort of girl who always would have.

There was a bit of a pause, like Rachel was gearing herself up to say something, then suddenly she burst out with, "Actually, I think I might have!"

I looked at her in surprise. "A boyfriend?"

She nodded, ecstatically. She had both hands clasped round her cocoa mug like it was some kind of sacred vessel.

"I think so," she said. Her face had turned bright pink. She was obviously dying to tell me about it. "It's this boy I met in a shop. I went and knocked over a bunch of stuff and he helped me pick it up and we sort of got talking and –" her face was all scrunched up and had turned from pink to a deep rose – "he asked me if I'd like to go out with him."

I said, "Blimey! That was quick work."

"We talked for absolutely *ages*," Rachel assured me.

"About what?" I couldn't imagine Rachel talking to a boy.

"Oh," she said, "I don't know. Everything."

"So are you going to go?"

"D'you think I ought?"

"It's up to you," I said. "Depends whether you fancy him or not."

A giggle forced its way out of her.

"You do!" I crowed, triumphantly. "You fancy him!"

Shaking with giggles, Rachel buried her nose in her cocoa mug.

"Admit it," I said.

She made a little squeaking sound, which I took to be an admission.

"Hm." I sat cross-legged, nursing my cocoa. I wondered what Fawn would say if I told her that Rachel had a boyfriend. She'd never believe it!

But there wasn't any reason Rachel shouldn't have. With her new short haircut she was really quite pretty. It was strange, all the same, to think of Rachel with a boy. This was the girl who got all excited playing Snakes and Ladders!

"What's his name?"

"Danny." She gave this beautiful smile as she said it. She now had a brown moustache on her top lip.

"Where's he going to take you?"

"I don't know. I thought maybe we might go and have a coffee?"

I said, "Coffee?" Having coffee is what my mum does when she meets her friends. I couldn't imagine Fawn ever going to *have a coffee*. Me and John Arthur never had. It wasn't exactly my idea of a date.

"He's Italian," said Rachel. "Italians like coffee."

"Do you like it?" I said.

Rachel crinkled her nose. "Not really. But it doesn't have to be coffee! It could be, like… Coca Cola, or something."

I said, "OK."

"So do you think I should go?"

"Don't see why not. But what about your gran? What would she say?"

"Oh, I wouldn't tell Gran!"

"Probably best not," I agreed. "Doesn't sound like the sort of thing your gran would approve of."

"Gran doesn't approve of anything," said Rachel. "Look, it's nearly midnight! You know what that means?"

I said, "The witching hour!"

"It's when we tell ghost stories and eat the last bit of our feast."

"Oh, please!" I said. "Not the sardines?"

"You have to," said Rachel.

"I don't remember them doing it in Enid Blyton," I said.

"No, it's in this other book I found… *Girls of the Ivy Green.* See?" She crawled forward and pulled a book from a pile on the floor. It was a hardback and looked like it had been written long before even my gran was born. The girls on the cover were wearing these old-fashioned tunics tied round the middle, looking like sacks of potatoes. Inside, in spidery old handwriting, it said, *To Cynthia on her 10th birthday, Love from Granny, June 1919.*

"It's nearly a hundred years old!" I said.

"Yes," said Rachel, "but a midnight feast is a midnight feast. It's *tradition*. You sit round telling ghost stories and eating sardines and condensed milk."

"And then getting sick."

"No! You won't get sick. You've got to try it. Here!"

She was busy opening the tin of condensed milk and peeling back the top of the sardines. She held them out to me. I recoiled.

"You first," I said.

"You are such a coward," cried Rachel. "There's nothing to it! Watch."

I watched as she dunked a sardine in the condensed milk and dropped it into her mouth. She chewed, contentedly.

"Mm, ah… lovely! Now you."

Well, I didn't get sick, but sardines and condensed milk is not a combination I would recommend. It is, in fact, utterly repulsive. Even Rachel gave up after her second sardine.

"Well, I think that's enough," she said. "Now we'll go to bed and tell ghost stories!"

We both had to sleep in Rachel's bed, all bunched up together. My last thought as I closed my eyes was, *I hope I don't have to get up in the night.* I really didn't fancy the idea of creeping down that dark passage knowing that Rachel's horrible old gran was sleeping just the other side of the wall. It was scarier by far than any ghost story.

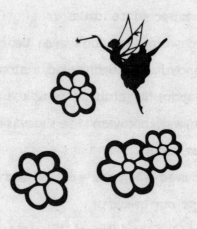

CHAPTER EIGHT

When we got up next morning the old witch woman was in the kitchen drinking what looked like a cup of hot water.

Rachel said, "Morning, Gran!" But she just got the usual grunt in reply.

I didn't say anything. I know Mum would have had

a go at me about manners, but I didn't see why I should be expected to make an effort when this horrible old woman couldn't even be bothered to open her mouth. She hadn't had a stroke and she didn't care about her husband dying, cos nobody had liked him, anyway, so it wasn't like she was in mourning. She was just rude!

I was relieved when she went off and left me and Rachel to get our breakfast.

"Is cereal OK?" said Rachel. "We could always have condensed milk with it."

I couldn't tell whether she was being funny or if it was a serious suggestion.

I said, "No, thank you!" and she giggled.

At ten o'clock Auntie Helen arrived.

"It's a pity you have to go," said Rachel. "I could have taken you into town and we could have looked for some more games. I saw one the other day called Monopoly. Do you know that one?"

I said, "Yes, I like Monopoly."

"I'll buy it!" said Rachel. "I'll keep it here for next time."

"Next time," I said, "you should come to mine."

The words shot out of my mouth before I could stop them. It was like an automatic reaction: I'd been to hers, so now I had to invite her back to mine. It's what you do. It's being *polite*. Except that I wasn't sure I really wanted Rachel coming for a sleepover. Not with Nat around. I wasn't exactly *ashamed* of Rachel, but there was no denying she was a bit different.

And then I saw that her face had flushed crimson with pleasure and I immediately felt bad. She had gone to such trouble, choosing all the food and searching for games that we could play. She had done her very best to give me a good time and I had enjoyed myself in spite of the games being for little kids. We had had fun! It was only right I should ask her back. Rachel couldn't be blamed for having a horrible old witch woman for a gran, any more than I could be blamed for having a stupid little sister. I could always have a word with Mum and get her to talk sternly to Nat beforehand. If Mum told her to behave herself, she would. Nat isn't a bad person, just a bit thoughtless.

Auntie Helen said that if I was ready we might as well be off. I wouldn't actually have minded going into town with Rachel but it was a bit too late to change my mind at this stage so I said "Thank you very much for having me" to the old witch woman and picked up my bag. The old witch woman, as usual, didn't say anything, though I think I might have heard her grunt again.

"Don't mind Auntie," said Auntie Helen, as we left the flat. "She's a woman of few words."

At the last minute Rachel came cantering down the hall saying that she would come with us.

"We're only going to the station," said Auntie Helen.

"Yes, but you could drop me off in town afterwards."

"I'll come back for you. You stay here and keep your gran company. She hardly sees anything of you these days."

Rachel's face fell, but she didn't argue. I wondered why she couldn't come with us. I couldn't imagine her gran being all that bothered whether she was there or not.

When we reached the station Auntie Helen said that my train wasn't due for another half-hour so she would park the car then come and wait with me in the station café. I tried saying that that was OK, I didn't mind waiting by myself – to be honest I would have preferred it cos sometimes I find it quite difficult to know what to talk about with grown-ups – but Auntie Helen insisted.

"The fact is, I wanted to have a word with you. About Rachel." She led the way into the café. "I can't tell you how happy I am that she has you for a friend! It was so lovely of you to invite her back. She's been looking forward to your sleepover for weeks. I do hope you enjoyed it."

I assured her that I did.

"I've been so worried about her, I can't tell you."

My heart sank. I thought, *Oh, please.* I didn't want to know! But Auntie Helen carried on.

"You're obviously close to her. You would know, if anyone would. Tell me, honestly… How is she doing?"

I mumbled that she was doing all right.

"Really?" Auntie Helen obviously wasn't quite sure whether to believe me or not. "Has she made any other friends besides you? You're the only one she ever talks about."

Triumphantly, cos that was something I could answer, I said, "Yes, that's cos we both had the chicken pox and started a week late!"

"So how does she get on with everyone else?"

"She gets on OK," I said. It was true, she *had* got on OK. Fawn and the others had been really patient with her. Until now.

"They don't find her… odd, in any way?"

I squirmed. I so didn't want to be disloyal to Rachel!

"You see, the reason I'm asking…" said Auntie Helen, "Rachel has had a very… well, I suppose you could say a very sheltered upbringing. Not exactly what you would call normal."

I suppose I'd already guessed that from seeing her horrible old gran.

"My uncle Stefan – that's Rachel's granddad – was a very controlling sort of person. Not to mince words, he was a bully. He bullied Rachel's gran, which is why she's like she is. Decades of being ground down. He bullied my dad. He bullied everyone he came into contact with."

I thought, *Why is she telling me all this?* What did she want from me?

"You've probably heard of God's Mission? No? Well, maybe not. It's a strict religious sect that believes in keeping as far away as possible from worldly temptations. When I was little, Uncle Stefan decided we should all go and live in this commune and be independent. So he moved us out to this big old house in Norfolk – my mum and dad and me, Rachel's mum, Rachel's gran, and another couple of families who'd fallen under his sway. Others joined us over the years. We were almost completely cut off from the rest of the world. No television, no computers. Nothing. Except for a radio, which belonged to Uncle Stefan. Nobody else was allowed to listen to it. He just passed on to us all the evil things that were happening in the world."

I really felt I ought to say something, but I couldn't think what. Fortunately Auntie Helen didn't seem to be expecting any response.

"It must be difficult," she said, "for you to understand why we all put up with it. I can only say that Uncle Stefan was not the sort of person you crossed. Not unless you were Rachel's mum."

A faint smile briefly lit up Auntie Helen's face, all big and plain and bony, but somehow reassuring.

"My cousin Ruth was the one rebel amongst us. She was the one that used to creep in and listen to the radio when Uncle Stefan wasn't around – until he found out and started keeping it under lock and key. She was always questioning… why this, why that? It used to make him so angry! Then when she was sixteen she ran away. We never got the full story of where she went or what happened, whether she fell in with a bad group of people, though if she did it was hardly her fault. What did she know? She'd had no experience. Anyway…"

There was a pause.

"Zoe, I'm really sorry," said Auntie Helen, "burdening you with all this. I know it's not fair. But you're Rachel's only friend, and you need to understand why it is if she sometimes seems a bit… different."

"OK." I sat up straight and did my best to look serious and intelligent.

"The fact is, my cousin Ruth ended up with a baby… Rachel. I remember she was terribly ill after the birth and we weren't allowed to see her. I begged and begged, but Uncle Stefan wouldn't budge. And then it was too late. She died, and we never got to say goodbye to her. I don't think Auntie Ellen ever got over it. Rachel's gran, that is. Things were just never the same after that. Uncle Stefan became even stricter. At least some of us were able to remember what normal life was like; we had at least experienced it. Rachel never had that chance. Not until now. You can imagine what an upheaval it's been for her. At the moment, she's still just trying to cope with ordinary everyday living. I'm sure she's finding it difficult – I know I am! But she's determined to get there. She wants so much to be like everyone else! She's not doing too badly, do you think? I mean, all things considered?"

Auntie Helen looked at me anxiously. I didn't know what to say. I couldn't believe she was telling me all this. I was only thirteen! But even I could see she needed to talk. So I just mumbled "Mm," in what I hoped was an encouraging sort of way. Auntie Helen's face lit up.

"She's trying so hard! It's barely a year since Uncle Stefan died and the commune broke up. You can't imagine! It was like being released from prison.

Everything was just so new and strange. A bit scary, actually."

Auntie Helen gave this small apologetic laugh. Like grown-ups aren't supposed to be scared. Or they're not supposed to admit it. But I didn't think any the less of her.

"By the end," she said, "it was just me and Rachel and her gran. Rachel so much wanted to go to boarding school! She'd read about it in these old books she had."

"Me too!" I nodded, enthusiastically, glad I was able to make a contribution at last. "That's what made me want to go."

"Well, all I can say is I'm extremely glad you did. I was so afraid that it was a mistake; that she'd never manage to make any friends. And she does so need them! Someone to understand and show her the way."

I wrinkled my nose, embarrassed. "Dunno if I'm doing that."

"Oh, but you are! She's so much more confident

than she was just a few weeks ago. I've been doing my best but really and truly –" Auntie Helen laughed again; that same little half-ashamed laugh – "really it's like the blind leading the blind. I've no more idea of what passes for normal than Rachel does. You can teach her; I'm just floundering. And her gran, of course, is no help. Just the opposite. It's all happened too late for her. That's why I thought it might be best for Rachel to go and board. Left at home with her gran – or even with backwards-old me – she'd never manage to break free. As it is, she's become almost rebellious! Getting her hair cut, for instance… You have no idea what a bold step that was."

"I hope she didn't get into trouble?" I said.

"Well, her gran wasn't best pleased, but Rachel's learning to stick up for herself. Like that trip to the theatre. A year ago she would never have been allowed. She still wouldn't have been if her gran had had her way."

"She was ever so excited," I said.

"What about the dress?" Auntie Helen said it eagerly. "She wanted something special to wear. Was it all right?"

I hesitated. What could I say? That awful yellow dress!

"It wasn't," said Auntie Helen, "was it?"

"It wasn't that bad," I said.

"It was! I can tell from your face. I do hope people didn't laugh at her?"

"N-no. They just sort of accepted that maybe she didn't know any better."

"But what do they think of her? Do they think she's… well, in any way… peculiar?"

"Different," I said. "But… you know! She's a Daisy."

"Ah, the famous Daisies! I've heard all about them. She's really proud of being one."

"It's only the name of our dorm," I said, "but we tend to stick together. We're doing Shakespeare scenes at the end of term. On stage. It's not supposed to be a competition, but we really want the Daisies to do well."

"I'm sure Rachel does too."

"She won't join in, though. Fawn's written her this really nice little part as one of the fairies in *A Midsummer Night's Dream* and she just won't do it!"

Sadly, Auntie Helen shook her head. "If you're asking her to get up on stage and act, then I'm afraid just at the moment that would almost certainly be a step too far. You have to remember, she's been brought up to believe that anything to do with the theatre is sinful. That's why it was such a breakthrough when she went on that school trip. But actually getting up on stage herself… she's not ready for that. There are just too many bonds that tie her to the past. She's doing her best, she really is, but we can't expect her to burst free of them all at once. I'm so sorry, Zoe, I know it's asking a lot of you, but you'll have to be patient."

Well, I thought, maybe *I* could be, now that I knew the reason for her strange behaviour, but I wasn't so sure about Fawn and the others. Not unless I could tell them the story.

I was about to ask Auntie Helen if that would be OK when she leaned forward, very earnestly, and said, "I must ask you, by the way, not to pass any of this on. I only told you because you're Rachel's friend, but she would be absolutely mortified if she knew."

I wasn't sure what mortified meant, but I guessed that for some reason it meant she would be upset. Auntie Helen explained.

"She so desperately doesn't want anyone to know. We had to explain to the school why she's never learnt anything about computers, but even they don't know the whole of it. If it had been up to me, I would have told them, but Rachel begged me not to. She got so upset! She just wants to be thought of as a normal regular person."

But she wasn't a normal regular person, and people were beginning to lose sympathy.

"I can trust you," said Auntie Helen, "can't I? Please, Zoe! Promise me you won't breathe a word."

Of course, I had to. What else could I do?

 159 ☆

"I realise," said Auntie Helen, "that it's a lot to put on your shoulders, and maybe I shouldn't have done it, but I do worry so about her. She's been through such a lot! And she depends on you so much."

I wriggled, uncomfortably. I didn't want to be depended on! I just wanted to get on with my life without all these complications. Auntie Helen glanced at her watch.

"Time to be going. Zoe, I want to thank you so much for listening to me! I feel a lot better now that I've met you."

As I sat on the train, I thought back over all that Auntie Helen had told me. It explained so much! Even a little thing that had subconsciously niggled at me ever since that first day we'd met, in the dorm, before the others had shown up, when I'd asked Rachel if she was Swedish and she'd said that her granddad had been.

"He was called Lindgren. That's why I am."

I hadn't really thought about it at the time, but later

it had come back to me and I had wondered what her granddad had to do with it. Her *granddad* had been called Lindgren. What about her dad? And now I knew why she'd never played Snap or seen a pack of cards. Why going to the theatre had been such a big thing. Why she had no dress sense. Why she knew nothing about computers. Why, so often, she seemed to be playing a part. It was like she'd been brought up in some kind of vacuum, totally shut off from society. Really, the more I stopped to think about it, the more I had to admire her for the way she was coping. If only I could explain to the others!

I'd hardly been home five minutes when my phone rang. It was Fawn, wanting to know how things had gone.

"Did you manage to talk some sense into her?"

I said, "No, but I honestly don't think it's her fault."

"What d'you mean, it's not her fault? All she's got to do is just learn half a dozen lines!"

"Yes, I know, but—"

"She still won't do it?" That was Chantelle's voice, loud and angry in the background.

"Did you really try?" said Fawn.

"I did! But—"

"Oh, stop making excuses!" That was Fawn again. "She's just gone and ruined everything and that's all there is to it."

Bang. End of conversation.

I couldn't help feeling that Fawn's reaction was a bit over the top, though maybe that was only because I knew things that she didn't. Looking at it from Fawn's point of view, I had to accept that Rachel probably just seemed to be letting everyone down.

Mum happened to be passing as I was talking to Fawn. "Trouble?" she said.

I heaved a sigh. "I don't know what to do!"

"Want to talk about it?"

I hesitated. It surely wouldn't do any harm to just tell Mum. When Auntie Helen had made me promise not to tell *anyone*, she'd only meant other people at school. Mum would never let on.

In the end I told her the whole story, the way Auntie Helen had told it to me. Mum listened intently.

"Oh, the poor girl!" she said. "Thank goodness she has you for a friend."

"But what do I do?" I wailed. "Auntie Helen asked me not to tell!"

"In which case you mustn't," agreed Mum. "Auntie Helen was right when she said it was a lot to burden you with, but she probably has no idea which way to turn. From what you say, she was just as much a victim as Rachel, and for far longer. She must be struggling too."

"She says it's like the blind leading the blind."

"I'm sure she's right."

"So what am I supposed to do?"

"I think all you can do," said Mum, "is stay loyal to Rachel and stick up for her as much as you can. I know it's a lot to ask, and it's not going to be easy, but if anyone can do it, you can."

I looked at Mum, wonderingly.

"Come on!" said Mum. "You're no shrinking violet. *Overweening confidence*. Remember?"

It was what one of my school reports had said. I hadn't known what *overweening confidence* meant. "Too cocky by half!" according to Dad. I suppose it is true that I sometimes go jumping in without thinking. But not this time! This time I had been *sworn to secrecy*.

"Don't worry," said Mum. "You'll be fine. Just do your best, you can't do more."

CHAPTER NINE

I did my best. I really did! But Fawn and Chantelle were so cross. Chantelle said they had spent hours over half term rewriting Fawn's script. I could feel for them. It is one thing to do ordinary revising, like we are always being told to do; quite another to be forced to go back and butcher something that you'd got just the way you wanted it.

"We had to pick it all to pieces," grumbled Fawn. "It's not simply a case of cutting lines."

"Or just giving them to other people," added Chantelle.

Humbly I said, "No, I can see that."

They weren't actually saying it was my fault, but I knew they all felt I hadn't done as much as I could to make Rachel change her mind. Even Tabs and Dodie were reproachful.

"She is supposed to be your *friend*," said Tabs.

They all got especially mad when I tried to stick up for her.

"If you say one more time that she can't help it, I'll scream!" declared Fawn.

"And why can't she help it, anyway?" That was Chantelle, all aggressive.

"It's the way she's been brought up," I pleaded.

"*What* way?"

"Well, like… home-educated?" I said. I couldn't see there was any harm in just saying that.

"So what?" Fawn turned on me, savagely. "Lots of people are home-educated. Stop making excuses!"

In the end, since sticking up for Rachel didn't really seem to be doing much good, and in fact if anything it was just making things worse and getting them all even angrier, I stopped doing it. There didn't seem any point when I couldn't properly explain *why* I was sticking up for her. If I wasn't careful, they would all turn against me and then I would be cast into outer darkness, just like Rachel. I couldn't see how that would be of any help to either of us.

Fawn declared that from now on we were going to rehearse at least three times a week and that when we weren't rehearsing we would be making costumes and "Bottom's head".

"Which I have decided," she said — she had become extremely bossy, but she was, after all, both the writer and the director, not to mention the star — "will be a mask rather than a proper head. Dodie's good at that kind of thing, aren't you?"

Dodie, modestly, agreed that she was.

"Right," said Fawn. "First rehearsal tomorrow and I want everyone to be word perfect!"

"Ooh, can I come?" begged Rachel, when she heard. "Can I come and watch?"

Fawn said, "No, you most certainly cannot! Rehearsals are strictly private."

"Only for people taking part," said Tabs.

"But you wouldn't even know I was there! I'd be quiet as a mouse."

"I said no," said Fawn. "It's my production, I'm the director, and I say we don't need any outsiders."

Rachel's face grew crimson.

"It's nothing personal," Dodie assured her, though of course it was. "It's just that it's a bit off-putting if there are people watching you before you're properly ready."

"At least I can help make the costumes," said Rachel.

But they wouldn't even let her do that.

"We don't *need* any help," said Chantelle. "We've got it all sorted."

I did my best to soften the blow.

"It's just that we're meant to do everything ourselves. It would be like cheating if we let you help, being as you're not part of it."

Rachel didn't say anything to that. I knew she was feeling hurt and upset, but what was I supposed to do? I couldn't even tell her that I understood what she'd been through. It would have helped if we could have talked about it, but Auntie Helen had sworn me to secrecy, so I had no choice. I am not good at keeping secrets at the best of times. They tend to come blurting out of me before I can stop them. So when Fawn and Chantelle were being especially nasty it took a real effort not to say anything.

I hated to see Rachel so downcast. I hated being the one in the middle, trying to be loyal to Rachel while at the same time staying friends with the others.

Above all, I hated the responsibility. I really almost wished that Auntie Helen hadn't told me.

On the Tuesday after half term, Rachel received a letter. Almost nobody ever got letters, unless maybe it was their birthday; it was all emails and texts. Or maybe Facebook, if, like Dodie and Chantelle, your mum and dad were abroad. I suppose we were all mildly curious when Rachel came bouncing in at morning break, pink and flushed and waving an envelope. Not that any of us would actually have shown it. Not even me. As for the others, they were all pretty well ignoring Rachel these days.

I watched as she carefully opened the envelope and pulled out a card. *Could* it be her birthday? Surely not, or she would have told me. A little excited squeak came out of her. And then she fell into a fit of the giggles and pressed the card to her lips.

Fawn looked across at her in some annoyance.

"What is it?" I said.

Rachel gazed at me, soulfully, over the top of the card.

"It's him… It's Danny!"

"Oh," I said. "You saw him?"

She nodded, ecstatically.

"You went for a coffee?"

"Not just a coffee." She giggled again and pressed the card back to her lips. "We're seeing each other!"

Fawn and Chantelle exchanged glances. I saw Fawn's lip curl. They were being totally unfair! Having a boyfriend was a bigger thing for Rachel than they could possibly imagine. I was just so pleased for her. Relieved too. She might be going through an unpopular phase at school, but at least in her private life she had something happening. It was more than I did! I hadn't had a sniff of a boyfriend since John Arthur.

"God," said Fawn, later, "she is such a drama queen! What's with all this *mwah mwah kissy kissy* stuff?"

"And a *boy*friend?" said Chantelle. "Where would she get a boyfriend from?"

"She bumped into him in a shop," I said. "She knocked some stuff over and he helped pick it up and they got talking."

"About what, for goodness' sake?" That was Fawn again. "What does Daffy possibly have to talk about? To a *boy*?"

I was at a bit of a loss myself. It was hard to think of Rachel and a boy – any ordinary sort of boy – having anything very much to say to each other.

"I wonder what he's like?" said Tabs.

"Some kind of nerd." Fawn said it scornfully. "Have to be, if he's going out with Daffy."

"To be fair," said Dodie, in an apologetic tone, "she is quite pretty, now she's had her hair cut."

"Yes, but she's totally loopy."

"Talking of boyfriends," said Tabs, "how's yours?"

"Jax?" Fawn brightened. She told us how she and Chantelle had been to a party at half term with Jax and his friend from school. "Crispin. He really fancies Chantelle!"

The talk swung on. I was left wondering what Nat and Dad would have to say about someone that was called Crispin. But then, what would they say about someone that was called Fawn? I reminded myself that you couldn't condemn people solely on account of what they were called. Fawn had been a bit of a shock when I first met her, but up until just a few days ago I had thought she was really nice, if a bit full of herself.

I did understand how important it was, the Daisies putting on a good show. Fawn was hugely competitive. If anyone was a drama queen, it was her! But more than that, she had gone to such trouble. *And* she had made sure that everyone had a real part, even those of us that couldn't act. It wasn't like she'd hogged all the best lines for herself.

And I really couldn't blame her for feeling sore now, any more than I could blame the others for taking her side. After all, they'd been friends for ages before Rachel and I had come along. But I did so wish I could tell them her story! Surely then they would understand and make allowances?

I tried talking to Dodie, just like *hinting* why Rachel couldn't help being the way she was, but Dodie said Fawn didn't mind her being all weird and peculiar, just so long as she was willing to be part of the team and do her bit to beat the Buttercups.

"It's a question of loyalty," she said. And then, being Dodie and really soft-hearted, she added, "I know you say she can't help it, and I'm really sorry if she's unhappy, but it's not fair to blame Fawn! She wouldn't ever let *anyone* down."

I gave up after that. I'd done what I could! Even Mum couldn't expect me to do any more.

What with one thing and another, mainly to do with the play, I saw hardly anything of Rachel except in class and at mealtimes. We didn't even travel back on the train together at the weekend, because Fawn wanted extra rehearsals and Mum had agreed I could stay over. I was so deliriously happy that just for a while I almost forgot about Rachel and her problems. I did ask her, as she left on Friday, whether she'd be seeing Danny and she said, "Yes, we're going to spend all day together."

I said, "All day? Wow!"

I should probably have asked her what they were going to do, but I was eager to get back to the others. Fawn wanted us to discuss costumes, and especially mine. Should we try making a real proper head or was it OK to just have a mask?

"See you Sunday," I said to Rachel. "Don't do anything I wouldn't!"

With that I went rushing off, comforting myself with the thought that Rachel was obviously going to have a good time and that things were going well with her and Danny. Maybe it would be OK if I stopped worrying about her for a bit.

I have to say that rehearsals were a lot of fun! Fawn was an excellent director, in spite of being so demanding and bossy – which maybe she had to be – and I really loved my role as Bottom.

"We are absolutely going to *thrash* those Buttercups!" said Tabs.

Rachel came back from her weekend looking mysteriously pleased with herself. Every now and again she would burst into sudden and unexplained giggles, little trills of laughter which she tried to stifle by clapping a hand to her mouth. Everyone but me pointedly ignored her.

"What happened?" I whispered. "Did something happen?"

She shook her head. "Can't say."

"Did he kiss you?"

Another burst of giggles. "Can't say!"

"*Drama queen.*" Fawn mouthed the words at me, over Rachel's head.

I shrugged my shoulders; at least she was happy. I refused to do any more worrying.

On Tuesday she had another letter. A large one, this

time. We all watched – pretending not to – as she peeled back the flap and slid out what looked like a photograph. She didn't do her squeaking thing, or press it to her lips; she simply sat there, like, transfixed, with this smile of pure bliss on her face. I couldn't help it: I had to ask.

"What is it?" I said.

"It's a photo," said Rachel.

"Of him?"

She nodded, ecstatically. "You said why hadn't I got any so I asked him and he promised to send me one. He must have done it the minute we said goodbye!"

Now even Fawn couldn't resist.

"So let's have a look!"

We all craned forward. With shy pride, Rachel held up her photograph. It was black and white, big and glossy. The head shot of a boy, smiling out at us. Dark hair, big melty eyes and the words *Rachel with love from Danny xx* scrawled across it in Day-Glo yellow.

We all fell silent. I think we were a bit taken aback.

In the end Fawn said, "Hm!" and rather pointedly started talking to Chantelle in this loud, penetrating voice about something else.

It was Dodie who said, "Nice!"

Rachel glowed, bashfully.

"Not bad," agreed Tabs.

The boy in the photo was more than not bad. He was what Debs, one of my friends at my old school, would have called *swoon material*. Seriously good-looking! But Fawn was obviously determined to put an end to any discussion before it could even get started.

"Me and Chantelle have decided," she said, "we're going to have a special costume fitting at four-thirty. OK?"

I didn't honestly think that a special costume fitting was necessary, but it was Fawn's show so you couldn't argue. We all agreed that we would be there.

"I've been having new ideas," said Fawn. "What I thought was…"

The conversation moved on, with Rachel and her photograph abruptly forgotten. She was left there, sighing over it, by herself. I felt bad, but every time I so much as glanced in her direction or leaned forward to say something, Fawn hauled me straight back in.

"What does Zoe think?" she would say. Or, "How does Zoe feel?"

After a while, I noticed that Rachel had quietly disappeared.

When we went up to the dorm later on, we found that she had stuck her photo on the wall above her bed, using lumps of Blu-Tack. It hit you in the face as soon as you came through the door.

"Well, that's stylish," said Fawn.

She wouldn't have said it if Rachel had been there. It was Fawn's policy now to act like Rachel didn't even exist. But the photo niggled at her, you could tell. She kept shooting these irritable glances at it when she thought people weren't watching. I knew what her problem was: she couldn't believe that the despised Daffy had managed to acquire a boyfriend better looking than hers. I'd seen pictures of Fawn's boyfriend. He might go to a posh school, but he wasn't anywhere near as gorgeous as Rachel's Danny.

I confess that I was a bit surprised myself. Like the others, I'd been expecting some kind of nerd, all goofy and dim, with glasses and sticking-out teeth. I know that is not the sort of thing you are supposed to say. Just because someone happens to wear glasses and has teeth that stick out doesn't mean they are any less worthy as a human being. I know this! But in spite of being transformed after her haircut, there was no denying Rachel was still… Well! Socially challenged is how I would put it. It wasn't her fault, but I really just couldn't see her getting on with a boy. I sometimes found it difficult enough myself and I'd been around them all my life.

That Friday after school, because Fawn had given us the night off from rehearsing, Rachel and I travelled back together. It was the first time we'd really had a chance to talk in days. Rachel had been subdued all week, but she perked up a bit when I started questioning her about Danny. It was obvious that she loved to talk about him. I asked her how old he was and she said sixteen. She said it like going out with a boy of sixteen was something to be proud of. Maybe it was. John Arthur had been in Year Seven, same as me, and Fawn's boyfriend, I knew, was only fifteen.

I said, "Which school does he go to?"

"Starlight Academy," said Rachel.

I blinked. "Where's that?"

"It's in Ipswich," she said. And then, with an air of suppressed importance, "It's a stage school."

"A *stage* school?" That took me by surprise. "You mean — he's an actor?"

She nodded, her cheeks all puffed and pink with happiness.

"I didn't say anything before, cos of not wanting to make Fawn jealous."

Excuse me? *Fawn?* Jealous of *Rachel?*

"He's in this series," said Rachel. "*Gangbusters.*"

"What, on TV?" I shook my head. I'd never heard of it.

"He's only just finished it," said Rachel.

"So when's it going to be shown?"

"I'm not sure, but soon as it is I'm going round to Auntie Helen's to watch it. Auntie Helen," said Rachel, "has a *television set*. Gran won't have one cos she says they're a tool of the devil. But Auntie Helen doesn't take any notice of what Gran says. She does her own thing."

"Tell me more about the series," I said. "What part does he play? What's it about?"

"I don't know," said Rachel. "It's a secret."

"So what's his surname?"

"Vitullo. Danny Vitullo."

"Has he done other things?"

"He's been in a show called *Peter Pan*. In London."

"Oh," I said, "I know *Peter Pan*! What part did he play?"

"Something called a Lost Boy?"

"Wow."

I was impressed! But I couldn't help feeling, as I got

off the train, that it was just as well Rachel *hadn't* mentioned anything to Fawn. It might not have made her jealous, but it would certainly have upset her. The thought of Rachel, of all people, having a boyfriend that was an *actor*. I could just hear her.

She can't take part in my play, but she's going out with someone at stage school?

For once, I thought, Rachel had shown a bit of discretion.

CHAPTER TEN

It wasn't till Dad had met me at the station and driven me back home that I discovered Gran was there.

"She's staying for a *fortnight*," announced Nat, all self-important because she'd known about it and I hadn't.

"Why didn't you tell me?" I wailed.

"We wanted it to be a surprise," said Mum.

"Like a surprise party," added Nat.

Gran held out her arms. "I just hope it's a nice one."

It couldn't have been nicer! I always love it when Gran is with us. She lives down south, in Dorset, and is very independent. We don't get to see her that often.

She gave me this big hug and I thought how different she was from the sour old woman that was Rachel's gran. I knew Rachel's gran had been crushed and squashed by her horrible husband, but after all she had *chosen* him. And she didn't have to let him treat her that way. I wouldn't ever let anyone!

"So how is school?" said Gran. "St Thingummy, or whatever it is."

"Beefburga!" chortled Nat.

Gran said, "*Beefburger?*"

"She thinks she's being funny," I said.

"*Beefburga, Cheeseburga—*"

"It's her idea of a joke."

"*Hamburga, veggieburg—*"

"Natalie, just be quiet," said Mum. "You're going to have your gran all week. Zoe's only got her at weekends."

"So whose fault's that?" said Nat. "Gran, did I tell you Lottie's got a new trick?"

"Show it to me later," said Gran. "We'll have plenty of time."

Nat went off in a bit of a huff. "Just have to hope she still remembers it!"

Gran said, "Well! What was that about?"

"It's all right," said Mum. "She's still not too sure how she feels about Zoe deserting her and going to what she calls 'a posh school'."

"*Is* it posh?" said Gran. "I suppose it has to be, if it's boarding."

Why did all my family have this hang-up about *posh*? All except Mum. She was the only one that was relaxed about it. *She* knew I wasn't going to get all snooty.

"I don't think your friend Rachel's particularly posh, is she?" Mum looked at me, enquiringly.

"Rachel's not posh *at all*," I said.

"How is she doing, anyway?"

I said, "She's got a boyfriend!"

"Who has?" That was Nat, trundling back with Lottie in her arms. She sank down next to Gran on the sofa. "Who's got a boyfriend?"

"Rachel," I said.

"Your funny-looking friend?"

I snapped, "She's not funny-looking!"

Nat leaned in close to Gran. "She's got white hair," she whispered.

"Yes, she's also got a boyfriend," I said. "More than you're ever likely to have!"

"More than you've got, an' all," said Nat.

"You don't know what I've got!"

"I c—"

"Girls, for goodness' sake!" said Mum. "Is this really necessary?"

I said, "Yes, if she's going to be rude about Rachel."

"Dear, oh dear," said Gran. "I wonder if I just ought to pack up and go home?"

That made us ashamed. We both subsided, Nat cuddling Lottie, me perched on the arm of Mum's chair.

Mum said, "That's better! Your gran didn't come here to listen to you two squabbling. Zoe, I'm really pleased for Rachel. Having a boyfriend must be doing wonders for her confidence."

"It is," I said. "She can't stop talking about him! He's an actor."

"An *actor?*" said Mum.

Nat made this rude honking noise down her nose. I looked at her, irritably. "What's that in aid of?"

Nat said, "Well! Honestly."

"Honestly what?"

"An *actor.*"

"So?"

"I bet you she's just making it up!"

"Why would you say that?" wondered Mum.

"Cos it's what this girl in my class did. Emily Harper. She told everyone her boyfriend was a pop star! Wasn't true," said Nat. "Just made her look stupid. She didn't half embarrass herself!"

"Poor little thing," said Gran. "She was obviously desperate to impress."

"More to the point," said Mum, "what is an eleven-year-old-girl doing with a boyfriend in the first place?"

Nat rolled her eyes.

"It's the times we live in," said Gran.

"I don't know." Mum shook her head. "How old is this boyfriend of Rachel's?"

I said, "Sixteen. He goes to a stage school in Ipswich. Starlight Academy?"

"Never heard of it," said Nat.

Well, and why would she? What did she know about anything?

"He's just made a TV series," I said.

Nat's head jerked up pretty fast when I said that. "What TV series?"

"Something called *Gangbusters*."

 189 ☆

Nat got as far as "Never—" when Gran suddenly burst out, excitedly.

"Oh!" she cried. "*Gangbusters!* That was on when I was young – I used to love it. All about these three teenagers working as secret agents. I can even remember their names… Steve, Mike and Jill. They must be doing a remake! I wonder when it's going to be shown?"

I promised that I would find out.

"Oh, please do!" said Gran. "I'll make a point of watching."

Later on, when we were by ourselves, Mum said, "I do hope Rachel's not going to get herself hurt."

"You mean because of her boyfriend?" I said.

"It sounds as if she's really fallen for him. But if he's a young actor…"

"You think he's just, like, playing her along?"

"No, not necessarily, but he must lead quite an exciting sort of life, being in a television series – especially if he's playing one of the main parts."

Rachel hadn't said what part he was playing.

"Maybe," I suggested, "he's just an extra."

"Even so, it's still exciting. And he's still at stage school! It's very different from being at an ordinary school."

I said, "Yes, I suppose." Except that if he was only an extra, that wasn't anything terribly special. It wasn't like extras had any lines to say or anything very much to do, except just rush around in a group. Thinking about it, I decided that's what Danny would almost certainly turn out to be: just an extra. That would account for Rachel not being able to tell me what part he was playing. Cos he didn't *have* a part. It didn't mean he wasn't an actor! Well, training to be.

Back at school, Rachel couldn't resist the temptation to boast. Now that I knew her secret, there obviously wasn't any reason for keeping it from the others.

"He's an actor," she said proudly, when she saw Fawn casting one of her glances at the photo.

I couldn't blame her. Danny was worth boasting about! But it got Fawn really niggled. Every time we entered the dorm and saw Danny's photo smiling down on us she went, "*Actor!*" in scornful tones. If Rachel was there, she mouthed it at us. Silent, but still scornful.

I said, "According to Rachel, he's just finished making this thing for television."

"What *thing?*" said Fawn.

"Something called *Gangbusters?* It's a remake! My gran used to watch it when she was little."

"Oh." Fawn's lip curled slightly. "A *children's* thing."

"It's still acting," said Dodie.

"I suppose. If it ever actually gets shown."

"Why wouldn't it?" I said.

"Well." Fawn shrugged. "It could just be a pilot. Sometimes they just do one episode to see how it works out and then they junk it. It's what actors say when they want people to think they've been doing something when really and truly they've just been out of work. *Resting*," she explained, for those of us who might be ignorant.

"Then when you ask a few months later why it's never been shown they go, 'Oh, it was pulled.' That means cancelled," she added. "And nobody can prove that it wasn't, cos I mean occasionally things *do* get cancelled. But other times it's just actors pretending."

I frowned. "You think Rachel's boyfriend is just pretending?"

"More likely *she's* just pretending," said Fawn. And then she did her little scornful laugh and went, "Actor!"

"It hardly seems very likely," agreed Chantelle.

I found it all a bit worrying, what with Nat and now Fawn. Anxiously, I asked Rachel if she was sure Danny didn't know when the show was going to be on TV.

"I hope it's not one of those they cancel," I said.

Rachel looked alarmed. "Why would they cancel it?"

"It's what they do! They make a pilot and if it doesn't work out they cancel it. Is that what Danny made? A pilot?"

"I don't know." Rachel put a finger in her mouth and nibbled at a piece of skin. "He's done ten episodes!"

"Oh! Well, in that case," I said, relieved, "it should be all right."

So much for Fawn! She didn't know everything, however much she liked to pretend that she did.

She had called a final dress rehearsal for Saturday morning, ready for the performance next week, so Friday night I was staying on at school again. Being so busy with rehearsals, not to mention helping out with costumes, meant I was seeing almost nothing of Rachel at all. Two Saturdays in a row I got to stay on at school, while Rachel went home by herself. She hadn't said anything about a date for Danny's TV series and I kept forgetting to remind her. On the second Saturday I remembered at the last minute, but I was too late. She had boarded the school bus and gone off to the station before I had a chance. She had become like a ghost just lately, sadly drifting about with nobody bothering to notice her. A sort of shadow.

Earlier in the week she'd had another card. I only

knew who it was from because I recognised the writing on the envelope: bright green and all in capitals. Otherwise I would never have guessed. Rachel had just given this little secret smile. No sighing, no squealing. Even Fawn couldn't have accused her of being a drama queen. It was hard to look back and remember how bouncy she had been at the start of term.

When we went up to the dorm on Friday evening we discovered that Rachel's precious photo had come loose and floated to the floor.

"Oh, look!" cried Fawn. "The actor's taken a tumble!"

I bent to pick it up.

"What's that on the back?" said Chantelle.

I turned it over. Someone had rubber-stamped it, *Starlight Academy*. And then underneath, typed on strips of gummed paper:

Danny Vitullo

Age: 16 years

Playing Age: 13–15

Hair: Dark

Eyes: Brown

Height: 5'4"

Build: Slim

Credits:

Slightly in Peter Pan, *London Hippodrome*

Steve in Gangbusters, *10 episodes, Eastern TV*

We all turned to look at Fawn. She shrugged. "Obviously a publicity shot. It's what agents send out to casting directors."

"So it's true," said Dodie. "He really is an actor!"

"I *said* he looked like one," crowed Tabs.

"That's right, you did," said Chantelle. "Give yourself a gold star!"

"I think Rachel ought to have a gold star," said Dodie. "I mean –" she took the photo from me and considered it, head to one side – "gorgeous, or what?"

Fawn said, "Huh!" And then, "Funny she doesn't mind going *out* with an actor…"

She didn't have to finish the sentence. We were

supposed to be a team, and Rachel had let us down. I wasn't sure that Fawn would ever forgive her.

The first thing I did when I arrived home on Saturday afternoon was triumphantly inform Nat that she had been wrong. I had proof!

You'd have thought she might at least say she was sorry, but all she did was start off again about this girl in her class that had told them her boyfriend was a pop star, like that took away any need to apologise. Before I could say anything, however, Gran appeared, looking pleased with herself.

"See what I've found!" She held out a book. "*The Castle of Adventure!* That's one you haven't got."

I said, "Ooh, thanks, Gran!" doing my best to sound enthusiastic. I hadn't the heart to tell her I'd grown out of Enid Blyton.

"We went into town," said Nat. "Me and Gran. Went round the charity shops."

Gran said, "Yes, and see what else I came across!"

"*Gangbusters!*" cried Nat.

Gran nodded. "I remember my mum buying me this book for my tenth birthday. They'd just shown the series on television, and then they brought out the book. See?"

She passed it across to me. It was an old paperback, a bit tattered and torn. On the front was a photograph of three kids: two boys and a girl.

"Steve was my favourite," said Gran. "I was really in love with him!"

"Which one's Steve?" I said. But I already knew. I didn't need Nat self-importantly jabbing a finger at him.

Gran sighed. "Isn't he just gorgeous?"

"Not bad," agreed Nat. "But why's his hair like that?"

"You mean styled," said Gran. "It was the fashion in those days. Oh, he was a heart-throb!"

Nat giggled. "I suppose I could go for him."

"Me too," said Mum, peering over my shoulder.

Nat prodded at me. "What d'you think?"

I swallowed. I didn't know what to think.

"I used to write his initials all over my school books," said Gran. "*DV*... Oh, he was so lovely! I'm afraid whoever plays him in the remake will have a hard job convincing me. I suppose it will be some trendy young man. Still, no doubt he'll appeal to you girls. You can keep the book if you want. I'm a bit too old for heartthrobs!"

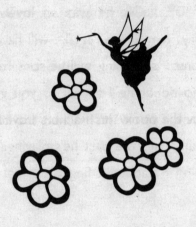

CHAPTER ELEVEN

I was very confused. My head was, like, spinning. I carried the book up to my room and sat there, on the bed, trying to make sense of what I was seeing. There had to be an explanation. There is always an explanation for everything. Tiny slivers of ideas went darting through my brain. Suppose... maybe –

It was no good. I still couldn't get it. I heard Mum coming upstairs and went out on to the landing. I said, "Mum…"

"Are you still swooning over Gran's heart-throb?" said Mum.

I held out the book. "It's Rachel's boyfriend," I said.

"You mean, that's the part he's playing?"

I said, "No." I stabbed a finger on the photo. "*This* is Rachel's boyfriend!"

There was a pause.

"This is the original cast," said Mum. She said it like perhaps I hadn't quite realised. "The book must be at least –" she opened it and glanced inside – "forty years old. They obviously did their best to find lookalikes."

"But, Mum," I said, "he's got the same name! It says on the back."

Mum turned the book over. "*Steve… Danny Vitullo.* That's the name of Rachel's boyfriend?"

I nodded.

"In that case, he must be his dad. You know these things run in families."

I did so want to believe her! But Mum could see that I didn't.

"You're not convinced," she said, "are you?"

I said, "Mum, I've seen his photo. It's the same boy!"

Mum studied me for a moment. "All right," she said. "Let's go and find out."

"How?" I bleated.

"How do you think?" said Mum. "The same way we find out everything these days!"

She led the way downstairs to the room Dad used as his office.

"OK. Let's put it into Google. *Danny Vitulo*. Was that how it's spelt?"

"Two 'l's," I said.

"*Vitullo*," typed Mum. "*Actor*," she added. "And there we are! Danny Vitullo. Let's see his Wikipedia entry. *Born 1946…*"

I said, "*1946?*"

"That's what it says. *Born 1946, died 1981.* Not very old. *Young actor, mainly remembered for his role as Steve in the Eastern Television series* Gangbusters. Died in a car crash. Not married." Mum looked at me, thoughtfully. "It seems you may be right. This *is* Rachel's boyfriend."

"But why?" I wailed. "Why would she do such a thing?" All that squealing and sighing. How could she? And there I'd been, defending her!

"Try not to be too hard on the poor girl," said Mum. "She's not the first person to spin stories about herself. I remember when I was at primary school I told everyone your gran was best friends with this famous woman that was a TV presenter."

"What, and she wasn't?" I said.

"She was her cleaner," said Mum.

I stared at Mum in amazement. "Mum! What made you do it?"

"Oh, I don't know! I suppose I wanted to feel important."

"Did they ever find out?"

"No, and if they had I'd have just died! So whatever you do," said Mum, "I don't think you ought to confront Rachel."

"You mean I just have to go on pretending?"

"I think you should do your best to let it die. Like, if she starts talking about it, don't ask her questions or do anything to encourage her. It's probably just a passing phase. The chances are she'll come back to school next term and it will all be forgotten."

"What I don't understand is where she got the photograph from," I wailed. "It's this huge great glossy thing with bits stuck on the back saying all about him, like how tall he is and how old he is and—"

I stopped. I knew where she had got the photograph! The same way she'd got most of her stuff. I remembered, the night I'd gone for a sleepover, pulling the box out from under the bed and Rachel snatching it back and telling me that those were her photographs.

I found them in one of those container things.

"She got it out of a skip," I told Mum. "She gets

everything out of skips, cos her horrible old grandmother won't let her buy things."

"So she must have come across his photo and begun to daydream. It's not unusual."

I thought that daydreaming was one thing. I daydream even now about beautiful Jez! But I wouldn't ever pretend he was my boyfriend. Not seriously. Maybe to myself; just now and again. Not to other people!

"I wonder if Starlight Academy still exists?" I said.

"Probably not," said Mum. "It was a long time ago. Let's put it in and see what comes up."

We discovered that Starlight Academy had been a children's drama school. It had opened in the 1950s and closed just recently, a few months ago.

"That would make sense," said Mum. "Obviously when they closed, everything was cleared out and dumped in a skip. But how dreadful that Rachel has to go grubbing about like that! I hope it makes you realise," she said, "how lucky you are."

I said, "Yes, Mum."

"I mean it," said Mum. Even back in the bad old days –" she meant before she and Dad had won the lottery – "you never had to get stuff out of skips. Charity shops, maybe. But digging around in other people's rubbish." She shook her head. "That is desperately sad. I can't help feeling it was fate that made you and Rachel both have chicken pox at the same time. I know you blame Nat for breathing over you, but from the sound of things Rachel really did need a special friend."

Yes, I thought bitterly, *if only it didn't have to be me!*

"Mum, we don't have to tell Nat," I said, "do we? Or Gran?"

Mum said, "We needn't tell Nat but your gran's not going to rest till she has a date."

"We could always say it's been cancelled," I suggested. "It's what they do, they cancel things! They do it all the time."

"Well, maybe," said Mum. "Or maybe I'll tell your gran the truth. She'll understand. She knows the whopping great lie I told about her and the television person!"

I arrived back at school on Monday morning to find Rachel hovering anxiously.

"*There* you are," she said.

I made a grunting sound.

"I wondered where you were!"

"It was the traffic," I said. "We got held up."

"I was beginning to think you weren't coming."

I said nothing to this, just pushed past her into school. She came flustering after me.

"I thought you might be sick or something."

"It was just the traffic."

"Auntie Helen's been sick. She's had this really bad c—"

"It was the TRAFFIC!"

I went storming on ahead of her, along the corridor. I didn't want to be late for class; they are very strict at St With's. I also didn't want to be lured into conversation with Rachel. How could she have lied to me like that? We were supposed to be friends! She hurried to catch up with me as we reached our classroom.

"I asked him," she hissed.

I didn't say, *Asked who?* I knew all too well who she was talking about.

"Danny," she said. "About his TV show? He's going to find out and let me know."

Fortunately I was saved from having to reply by the arrival of Mrs Blair, our form tutor. I really *really* didn't want to have to talk to Rachel about her mythical boyfriend. It was even worse than Nat's story about the girl who pretended her boyfriend was a pop star. At least she'd *had* a boyfriend. Rachel's was just totally made up. All that stuff about bumping into each other in a shop. And sending cards to herself! And the big glossy photograph with *Love from Danny.* How could she?

For the first two lessons I very studiously kept away

from her, as well as I could. We usually sat next to each other, but one of the Days was off sick so I quickly zipped across the room and slid into her empty seat. I knew Rachel would be hurt, and probably wondering what she'd done to upset me, but how are you supposed to react when someone will *insist* on talking about a boyfriend that doesn't even exist? I couldn't just keep on grunting or changing the subject.

The bell rang for morning break and I could see Rachel dithering by the door, waiting for me. I was quite relieved when Fawn grabbed me by the arm and yanked me back, saying, "Hey, Zoe!" She obviously wanted to get me on my own, without Rachel.

"Listen," she said, "Friday after the performance…" THE PERFORMANCE! It really meant a lot to Fawn. "My mum and dad are coming to pick us up and take us out for a meal. All of us! They'll bring us back afterwards, but it probably means you'd have to spend the night in school, unless your dad wouldn't mind collecting you really late, like nine o'clock or something. Will they let you come? D'you think it'll be OK?"

"No problem!" I said. "I'll just call to make sure."

I was so excited to be included. The others had been friends since Year Seven. And now I was one of them!

"Us lot have all got permission," said Chantelle. "We always have permission to go places with Fawn's parents."

"I'll get permission," I said. "I'll call Mum this evening!"

"Tell her you've absolutely got to come, cos it's a celebration."

"Like a wrap party," said Fawn.

I said, "*Rap* party?"

"Wrap! Like all wrapped up. It's what they do when they finish making something for TV… they have a wrap party."

Fawn knew everything there was to know about television. Like other people might say, "I'm going to be a teacher," or "I'm going to be a doctor," Fawn always said that *she* was going into television. She was either going to be an actor or a director. One or the other; maybe both. None of us doubted that she would.

Talking of television made me think – not that I wanted to – about Rachel.

"You did say we're all invited?" I said.

"Yes! All of us."

"Even Rachel?"

An expression of disgust appeared on Fawn's face. She said, "You must be joking! You think I'm going to ask *her*?"

"All of us just means *us*," said Chantelle. "She's not one of us!"

I couldn't honestly blame them. All the same, when we turned to leave the room and I caught sight of Rachel's face, pale and stricken, at the door, I felt a pang of real anxiety. So, obviously, did Chantelle.

"You don't think she heard?"

"Oh, so what if she did?" Fawn tossed her head. "She's only got herself to blame. We put up with all the embarrassment, like the hair and that awful dress, making us look like total idiots, and then she goes and does this! What does she expect? We have yet to discover," added Fawn, rather sourly, "what Miss Seymour will say when she finds she's not taking part. It was meant to be all of us."

"We could always say she helped behind the scenes," I suggested. "Cos, I mean, she would have done."

Fawn gave me a look of extreme irritation. "Don't keep making excuses for her!"

I protested that I wasn't. "I was just *saying*—"

"Well, don't!" snapped Fawn.

Thinking about it later, it came to me that Fawn was probably feeling a bit guilty. After all, Rachel *had* offered to help, like with the costumes, for instance. It was just that Fawn had been so angry she had refused to let her.

I didn't get to speak to Rachel for the rest of the

day; I hardly even saw her. It was like she was deliberately avoiding us all. Even Chantelle noticed.

"I do hope she didn't hear!"

She sounded worried, which quite surprised me. I'd never thought of Chantelle as being sensitive. She was always so upfront and aggressive. She looked at me, almost pleadingly.

"I don't think she can have done, do you? I mean, not unless she has ears like a bat."

I wasn't so sure, and I could tell that Chantelle wasn't, either.

"I know she's brought it all on herself, but she is kind of pathetic."

"It's not her fault," I said.

"You keep saying that!"

"Yes, because it's true. Honestly," I said, "she can't help being the way she is."

"Hm." Chantelle frowned. I thought for a moment she was going to relent. Maybe even have a word with Fawn. Surely Fawn would listen to her best friend? "I dunno." She shook her head. "You can't keep making excuses for people. I think you should go and talk to her. Go and tell her it's nothing personal."

But it was! Rachel hadn't been invited cos Fawn didn't want anything more to do with her.

"Tell her it's a wrap party. Just for members of the cast."

I said, "If she heard us, she'll already know."

"But if she didn't hear us, she's bound to find out and then she'll wonder why she hasn't been invited. You should definitely," said Chantelle, "go and tell her."

But I didn't want to!

"I don't see that it would hurt to invite her," I said.

"Fawn won't. She's still really cross."

"That's not right," I said. "People shouldn't bear grudges."

"No, and people shouldn't let people down," said Chantelle. "This means a *lot* to Fawn."

I sighed. I knew that it did. It was more than just

being in competition with the others. As far as Fawn was concerned, it was a matter of professional pride.

"D'you think by next term she'll have forgiven her?" I said.

Chantelle shrugged. "Dunno."

If she did, it wouldn't be so bad. After all, we broke up in a few days' time.

"She still won't be one of us," said Chantelle. "Not like you are."

For just a few seconds I glowed; but then she went and ruined it.

"You're going to have to decide," she said. "You know that, don't you?"

I looked at her, alarmed. "What d'you mean?"

"Well –" Chantelle shrugged – "it's obvious, isn't it? It's either her or us. You can't expect to go on being one of us *and* stay friends with Daffy."

And then I said it. The words came blurting out before I could stop them: "I'm not really friends with her!"

"She thinks you are," said Chantelle.

Auntie Helen did too. Auntie Helen was depending on me. She thought I was looking out for Rachel. So did Mum. Mum had told me to stay loyal. Denying that I was friends with Rachel wasn't loyal.

Oh, why did life have to be so complicated? I just wanted to be left alone to do my own thing!

CHAPTER TWELVE

"Here, Daffy!"

We were in the dorm the next morning, bed-making and generally tidying up, which was what we always had to do straight after breakfast. Chantelle had obviously been down to fetch the post. She sent an envelope skimming across the room on to Rachel's bed.

"One for you!"

I deliberately kept my gaze turned the other way. I wasn't sure I could bear to watch, especially if we were going to be treated to the usual big production, all sighings and swoopings. This was somebody who was actually *sending letters to herself.* How crazy was that?

I concentrated on neatly folding clothes and putting them away. In Enid Blyton they'd had servants for that sort of thing, but here at St With's we were expected to do it ourselves. I'd been quite surprised, at first. I'd even remarked on it to Mum and Dad. Dad, in his Dad-like way, had said he was "very glad to hear it". According to him it would be disgraceful to think that teenage girls had people clearing up after them, to which Mum had given a bitter laugh.

"Why not?" she'd said. "They do at home."

That is so not true! I always pull the duvet up after I get out of bed. I may not be quite as tidy as I am at school, but at school it is one of the rules, and they are very strict about it. In any case, it is more fun when you are doing these menial tasks with other people.

I turned to cram my hockey socks into a drawer. They were a bit muddy, but that was OK, it was almost the end of term.

I heard Dodie, in tones of wonderment, say, "Not even going to open it?" and looked round to see Rachel rather grimly stuffing her letter into her book bag.

"Isn't it from your boyfriend?"

That was Dodie again. I could tell she was trying very hard to be friendly. She was obviously feeling bad about Rachel not being invited to the wrap party.

Normally if anyone had spoken to Rachel about her boyfriend – her *so-called* boyfriend – she would have responded with a delighted giggle. Today she just made a kind of choking sound and rushed out of the dorm. Dodie looked bewildered.

"What?" she said. "What did I say?"

"Who knows?" said Fawn. "Just be thankful we didn't get all the drama-queen stuff."

"But I didn't mean to upset her!"

"Don't worry about it," said Fawn.

It is simply no use telling a sweet person like Dodie not to worry. It is going against her nature.

"You don't think –" the question was addressed to me – "you don't think they've broken up, or something?"

I didn't know what to think. How can you break up with an imaginary boyfriend? Or if you do – if you suddenly come to your senses and decide that enough is enough – why would you find it upsetting? More of a relief, I would have thought. Kill him off before anyone finds out.

"Do you think I should say something?"

Dodie was still appealing to me. I was Rachel's friend! I ought to know what the problem was if anyone did. But I didn't.

"Maybe we should just leave her," I said.

Dodie looked at me, doubtfully.

"Hey!" Tabs gave a sudden cry. "I just realised…"

She pointed, dramatically, in the direction of Rachel's

cubicle. We all swung round to see what had caught her attention.

"Omigod!" said Chantelle. "It's gone!"

The big glossy photograph of Danny had disappeared.

If I hadn't left a book on my bedside locker, I wouldn't have had to go back to the dorm at lunchtime to collect it.

And if I hadn't gone back to the dorm, I wouldn't have discovered Rachel, sitting frozen and cross-legged, on her bed.

Obviously we are not supposed to leave books on our lockers, we are supposed to bring everything we need into school with us. As Ms Pringle said when I asked permission to go and fetch it, "If you'd tidied up properly, Zoe, this wouldn't be necessary." We are not allowed back to the dorm until bedtime without asking one of the teachers, so it was quite a shock to find Rachel there. I didn't reckon anyone would have given her permission just to come and *sit*.

"What are you doing?" I said. I could hardly pretend not to have noticed her. "Did you get permission?"

She didn't say anything to that; just hunched a shoulder. I picked up my book.

"I came to get this. For English," I added.

Rachel made a small grunting sound by way of acknowledgement. I hesitated. I really *really* didn't want to ask her what was wrong. I knew what was wrong! She'd obviously heard Fawn inviting us all to the wrap party. All of us except Rachel.

You must be joking! You think I'm going to ask HER?

If I'd heard someone talking about me like that, I'd probably be sitting frozen on my bed. But I so didn't want to get into conversation!

I sidled towards the door.

"Are you coming down?" I said.

She shook her head.

"You'll get into trouble," I warned her, "if anyone finds you here."

Even that didn't have any effect. Generally speaking,

Rachel was a model of good behaviour. *She* never left books in the dorm or got told off for talking in class. She was always very anxious not to break the rules.

I stared at her, helplessly. I was tempted just to leave her sitting there and go back into school. But I kept hearing Auntie Helen's voice, *I can't tell you how happy I am that Rachel has you for a friend!*

I heaved a heavy sigh.

"Is something wrong?" I said.

Rachel bent her head.

"What is it?" I said. "Is it…"

Is it because of the wrap party? is what I'd been *going* to say. Instead, what came out was, "What's happened to your photograph?"

Why? Why? Why did I say that? I didn't want to talk about the photograph! To my horror, Rachel's eyes immediately filled with tears.

"It's over," she whispered.

Excuse me? *Over?*

"You mean —" I waved a hand — "you mean you're not together any more?"

"He's found someone else."

I swallowed. I couldn't think what to say.

"One of the girls at his drama school," said Rachel. She smeared the back of her hand across her eyes. "He told me at the weekend."

If I hadn't known the truth, I would actually have believed her. I almost *did* believe her! She made it sound so convincing.

Weakly I said, "I thought you had a letter from him just this morning?"

The tears came spilling out again. "That was to tell me he was sorry!"

I swallowed again. "I see." Not that I did, but I had to say something. Rachel was obviously in a state, even though it was all completely made up. "I'm sure you'll find someone else," I said. I almost added, *Maybe next time it'll be someone real*, but that would have been unkind. Plus I had this feeling that it could be dangerous, trampling all over a person's fantasy.

"I really think you should come back down," I said. "You can't stay up here all afternoon. And what about lunch? Did you have any?"

"Didn't feel like it."

I thought I'd missed her in the refectory. I thought she'd just taken herself off to another table, what with Fawn and the others being so unwelcoming.

"Please, Rachel," I said, "dry your eyes and come back into school. You'll find someone else, I promise you will!"

I managed to get her back in time for the first lesson of the afternoon, which was English, but she sat in the one empty desk as far away as possible from me and Fawn and the rest of us. I found it almost impossible to concentrate. I kept glancing across at Rachel to check she wasn't crying again.

I didn't *think* that she was, though from where I was sitting it was hard to tell. Miss Seymour said, "Rachel!"

and I saw her start like she wasn't quite sure where she was or what she was supposed to be doing. Very politely Miss Seymour suggested that perhaps she might like to carry on reading from where Tabs had left off.

"If it's not too much trouble?"

In this faltering voice, Rachel began to read. Reading out loud was something she was usually quite good at. Today she did nothing but fumble and fluff. I saw Fawn roll her eyes and Dana and her friend Maddy pull faces at each other. I wanted to stand up and shout, "Stop it! She can't help it!"

Because it was all falling into place. Rachel had been unhappy for so long. Ever since Fawn and the others had started to turn against her. That was when it had all started. I thought back to the night I'd stayed at her place, when we'd been in the bedroom, sipping cocoa, and Rachel had asked me if I had a boyfriend. I'd told her about John Arthur, and how we'd gone out for a bit. That had led us to talking about Fawn. Rachel had said, "I bet she's got one," and I'd said, "Oh, well, Fawn!"

Like, *She would have*. And then Rachel, all pink and excited, had come bursting out with her big news: she might have a boyfriend too!

Had she just suddenly decided? Or had she been planning it? And if so, why? What had made her do it? Did she really think it would impress Fawn and the others? That they would think more of her? I could have told her it wouldn't work. If anything, it had just irritated Fawn even more. The thought of Daffy, of all people, having a boyfriend that was a) gorgeous and b) an actor! It was like trespassing on Fawn's private territory. *She* was the theatrical one. *She* was the one that had gorgeous boyfriends.

I wondered what had made Rachel take her photograph down. She had been so proud of it! She could have kept the story going at least until the end of term. Nobody had ever suspected the truth. (Apart from Nat, who didn't count.) And while it was definitely a bit weird, making up an imaginary boyfriend, I could sort of understand why she'd felt the need to do it. I could even – just about – understand how a person could come to believe in their own fantasies. I sometimes had fantasies about bumping into Jez Delaney at one of his rock concerts and him asking me out. (I wish!)

What I couldn't understand was why all of a sudden, for no apparent reason, Rachel had decided to bring it all to an end and make herself even more miserable than she already was. I also couldn't really understand why it *was* making her miserable. Even if she'd come to believe that she actually *did* have this gorgeous boyfriend, she couldn't seriously believe he'd ditched her in favour of someone else? That didn't make any sense at all!

I gazed across the room at Rachel's bent head as she stumbled her way through *Jane Eyre*. That was when it came to me. A flash of what I think is called *insight*. Could it be that she had killed off her big romance to give herself an acceptable reason for being so unhappy? Cos maybe the *real* reason – Fawn and the others turning their backs on her, not inviting her to the party – was just too painful? Or too embarrassing, or too humiliating. Or maybe all of those things together.

I could still remember how I had felt, back in Year Six, when I had had this huge great row with a girl called Denice Robbins, who had once been my friend. She'd accused me of spreading lies about her, which I absolutely hadn't been. But she'd got it into her head that I had. She'd screamed at me that I was a horrible person and she didn't ever want to talk to me again. When I got home I was all quiet and subdued, which is something I never am, and Mum had been quite anxious and asked me what was wrong.

"What on earth has happened?"

I couldn't bring myself to tell her. It is very belittling to admit that people think you're horrible and won't talk to you. Instead, I'd pretended I was upset cos I'd broken the clasp on the little silver bracelet that Gran had given me for my birthday. Mum couldn't understand it.

"For goodness' sake, is that all? We can easily get it mended!"

As far as she was concerned, it was just one great big fuss over nothing. Galloping hordes of wild horses wouldn't have dragged the real story out of me.

So maybe, I thought, it was the same with Rachel. Maybe her imaginary boyfriend fancying another girl was her way of hiding the real problem? Maybe she thought that when people found out they might even feel sorry for her and stop being so mean? Because they *were* being mean. Fawn, mainly, but where Fawn led, the others followed.

I switched my gaze away from Rachel and transferred it instead to the back of Fawn's head, directly in front of me. Even the back of her head looked poised and full of confidence. It was so easy to be confident if you were Fawn. Someone like Rachel didn't stand a chance. And yet she had tried so hard! She'd come bouncing into school at the start of term, all bright and eager, just wanting to be liked and to fit in. Now it had all fallen to pieces and I, who was supposed to be her friend, hadn't helped her one little bit. I'd just felt resentful and blamed Nat for giving me the chicken pox, and even Rachel herself for making demands.

"We will be best friends," she'd said, "won't we?"

What was I supposed to say? *No?*

Saying no would have been rude and unkind, but if I really hadn't wanted to be friends, I could have found ways of discouraging her. Instead – as I was forced to remind myself – I'd actually been only too happy to agree. Of course we'd be friends! I might not have been too sure about *best* friends, but I'd certainly been grateful to have *a* friend. It was only later, when she started to embarrass me, that I'd got all resentful.

Even after I'd discovered *why* she was embarrassing, I didn't do anything very much to stick up for her. Just mumbled that she couldn't help it, then immediately backed down when Fawn got irritated. I'd always been more anxious to stay in Fawn's good books than to defend Rachel.

I was still contemplating the back of Fawn's head when Fawn turned round to look at me. She raised both eyebrows as if to say, *Well?* That was when I became aware that Rachel's voice was no longer droning on and that another voice – Miss Seymour's – was rather sharply addressing me.

"If you could possibly bring yourself to return to us, Zoe?"

Fawn shook her head, reprovingly. I thought, *She can be so smug at times*. She had absolutely no idea what it was like to be an ordinary mortal with a dad who was a handyman (even if he *had* won the lottery), let alone what it was like to be Rachel, isolated from the world by a mad and horrible granddad that crushed people and wouldn't even let her listen to the radio or play harmless games like Snakes and Ladders.

Miss Seymour said, "Zoe?"

I snatched at *Jane Eyre* and prayed I was on the right page. Fawn sucked in her lips as a sign of disapproval. I knew what her problem was: she was terrified Miss

Seymour would put my name in the order-mark book and that come the end of term we would lose out to the Buttercups. Last term, she had already proudly informed me, we had had fewer order marks than either the Buttercups or the Days. Why did she have to be so *competitive* all the time?

"Zoe, if you're ready?" said Miss Seymour. "We don't have all day."

"Sorry," I said. "I lost my place."

Fawn gave me such a look. But my mind was made up: I was going to have to say something. I couldn't let things go on like this!

CHAPTER THIRTEEN

I didn't want to say anything to Fawn any more than I'd wanted to talk to Rachel. Not that I actually *had* talked to Rachel; I'd been too much of a coward. I have to confess that I was almost a coward again. I got as far as saying, "Hey, Fawn…" and then couldn't bring myself to go on.

Fawn said, "What?" in a tone that didn't strike me as particularly encouraging.

An unworthy thought flitted through my brain. Suppose I *didn't* say anything? Maybe Rachel would decide she didn't like it at St With's and would ask Auntie Helen if she could go somewhere else. It's no good pretending I wasn't tempted. Life would be so much easier without Rachel!

"Did you want something?" said Fawn.

I opened my mouth – and then promptly shut it again. Fawn wasn't used to anyone challenging her. Not even Chantelle. She was going to be so angry! I could just hear her.

If you'd rather be friends with Daffy than with us, feel free!

And then what would I do?

"Speak!" said Fawn.

I was on the point of backing down. *Again.* It was only the sight of Rachel, sitting at a table on the far side of the refectory, sadly eating her teatime bread and jam all by herself, that gave me the courage to go on. I took a breath.

"Can I talk to you about Rachel?" The words came spluttering out.

Fawn raised her eyebrows. "Daffy?" she said. "What about her?"

Already there was a hint of irritation in her voice.

"Please, *please*, invite her to the wrap party!"

"Why on earth would I do that?" said Fawn. She sounded genuinely surprised. That I should dare to ask!

"Yes, why should she?" said Chantelle.

Dodie and Tabs had both stopped eating. I could see their eyes darting to and fro across the table, from me to Fawn and back again.

"Well?" said Fawn.

I swallowed. Not bread and jam, but a lump in my throat.

"She's so unhappy and I think she's been punished enough!"

The eyes flicked back to Fawn. Even Chantelle was looking at her, waiting to see how she would react.

"I'm not *punishing* her," said Fawn. "I just don't want anything to do with her. You can, if you want. No one's stopping you; it's your choice. Her or us. Up to you to decide."

My heart sank.

"It's not her fault," I said.

"Oh, will you just stop *saying* that?" Fawn thumped on the table with her fist. Heads all round turned to stare. "It's all I ever hear... *It's not her fault, she can't help it.* I don't *care* about her not being able to help it. I just care that she let us down."

"And why can't she help it, anyway?" said Tabs.

"*Don't.*" Fawn jabbed a finger in the direction of Tabs's face. Tabs recoiled, hastily. "Don't ask! I don't want to know. Just drop it, OK? She makes me so angry, I can't tell you!"

"Don't need to tell us," said Chantelle. "We can see for ourselves."

Fawn turned a furious gaze upon her. "Are you saying it doesn't make *you* angry? All that work we did, and all for nothing?"

"I was angry at the time," said Chantelle. "I guess I've kind of got over it, now."

Fawn stared, like she couldn't believe what she was hearing. This was her best friend, turning against her?

"Are you saying we ought to just forget about it?"

Chantelle shrugged.

"Just invite her along like nothing ever happened?"

"We can't go on ignoring her for ever," pleaded Dodie.

Fawn spun round. "Why not?"

"Well, because it… it wouldn't be kind!"

"*Kind?*" Fawn spluttered. "I don't feel like being kind! She doesn't *deserve* anyone being kind. Look, just shut up about her! I've had enough."

Chantelle caught my eye and pulled a face like, *What can you do?* I had this feeling that if it weren't for Fawn, the others might be ready to forgive and forget, as my gran would say. But Fawn is one of those people, the more she feels under attack, the more she digs her heels in. She wasn't ever going to budge. I suddenly had this vision of her mum and dad turning up on Friday in their massive great people carrier and the five of us joyfully bundling into it, leaving Rachel to make her solitary way home. Back to that dark, spooky flat, and the creepy old grandmother lurking in the corner like a spider in its web.

I'd never be able to enjoy myself! I'd be thinking of Rachel the whole time. Determinedly, I crammed my last piece of bread and jam into my mouth and pushed back my chair. There was only one thing for it. I'd tried tackling Fawn and it hadn't worked. Now it was up to me. As Fawn had said, it was my choice.

"Her or us. Up to you to decide."

There wasn't really any decision to be made. Sometimes it's just blindingly obvious what you have to do. I had to tell Rachel that I wasn't going to the wrap party after all. I'd make some excuse, like it was all a bit too grand, what with Fawn's dad being some big-shot businessman and her mum having her photo taken at Ascot in a big stupid hat with feathers all over it. I'd tell her I wasn't used to that sort of thing, which of course I wasn't. It would have been interesting, and Mum would have loved to hear about it, but on the other hand it would only upset Dad, so maybe just as well if I wasn't there. I'd probably make an idiot of myself, anyway. Me and my *overweening confidence*. I'd be bound to open my mouth and say something stupid.

Quickly, before my resolve could falter, I swore this sacred oath: *You will tell Rachel you are not going.* Instead, I decided, I would invite her back for a sleepover. Apart from anything else, I owed her. And maybe, if I could just stop brooding over all the fun that I was missing, I would even quite enjoy it. What was more important was that Rachel would enjoy it. I would make sure that she did!

It wasn't till almost suppertime that I saw her. She'd disappeared immediately after tea and I hadn't been able to look for her, as I'd promised Dodie I'd help put the finishing touches to the mask she'd made for my part as Bottom. We were on our way back to the common room for the last fifteen minutes before the supper bell when Rachel appeared. I was about to drag her off, saying I wanted to ask her something, when to my surprise Fawn suddenly elbowed her way past me.

"Daffy," she said, "we need to talk."

I could see Rachel flinch. She obviously thought Fawn was going to have a go at her. I have to say that I did too.

"Listen," said Fawn, "you know we're having a wrap party on Friday, after the performance?"

Rachel nodded, nervously.

"I've been trying to think of a way to include you, cos it would be *so* much nicer if we were all in it. I know you don't want to act, but I was wondering… I don't suppose you could do the introduction for us? Just say a few words? It wouldn't be acting! Look, I've written something down. Shall I read it to you? *The Daisies are* proud to present a scene from Shakespeare's *A Midsummer Night's Dream recreated by Fawn Grainger, who plays the part of Titania. Oberon is played by Chantelle Adebayo, Bottom by Zoe Bird, and Moth and Mustard Seed by Tabitha Rose and Dodie Wang. We hope you will enjoy it.*"

There was a pause.

"What do you think?" said Fawn. "We'd be ever so grateful!"

I prayed, silently. *Please, Rachel, please say yes!*

The others were all watching; they seemed as anxious as I was. The last thing I had ever expected was that Fawn would have a change of heart. Chantelle caught my eye and pulled an anguished face. I think we both knew that if Rachel said *No*, that would be an end of it as far as Fawn was concerned.

I saw Dodie gnawing on her bottom lip and Tabs with her fingers crossed. *Please, Rachel, please!*

"It would make such a difference," said Fawn. "You don't even have to learn it, if you don't want to. You could just read it, if that makes things easier."

A shy beam spread itself across Rachel's face.

"I can learn it," she said.

"*Really?* Oh, that is brilliant!"

There are times when you can't help but admire Fawn. She was making it sound as if having Rachel do the introduction was the one thing that had been missing. The one thing we were desperately in need of.

"Now all you have to do," she said, "is get permission to come with us on Friday."

"She'll come," I said. I would make sure of it!

Our Shakespeare scene went really well. So well that even Fawn didn't have any complaints. We weren't supposed to be in competition with the others, so we didn't officially win or get a prize or anything like that, but everyone seemed to agree that ours was THE BEST. People kept coming up and congratulating us. Elinor Gaynes, one of the prefects, said it was the most polished performance she had seen.

"Almost professional!"

Miss Seymour added that it had been an excellent idea to have Rachel perform the introduction. "A very nice touch."

Fawn basked, and Rachel positively glowed. She spent the rest of the afternoon and most of the evening with this great soppy smile on her face. I hadn't seen her so happy in a long time.

The wrap party was fun, even if I did keep looking at Fawn's mum and seeing her in her big feathery hat, which made me want to giggle. It was most probably nerves on account of me being sat next to Fawn's dad, who is a bit scary. He has this deep booming voice and this big jutting jaw. The sort of man that is always being interviewed on television as Someone Important. Try as I might, I couldn't imagine him and my dad together. They wouldn't have anything to talk about, except maybe golf, which was something Dad had recently taken up. Rachel, on the other hand, found loads to say. She was sitting opposite and they had this long chatty conversation all about newts and toads and tadpoles. I was impressed! I asked her afterwards how she knew about such things and she said, "We used to have a pond in the garden."

"Not where you are now?" I said.

"Where we were before," said Rachel.

I was hoping she would tell me a bit more, but she obviously wasn't ready yet, and I knew I mustn't push her.

It was almost half-past nine when we arrived back at school after the wrap party. Dad was there to collect us both and bring Rachel back to spend the night. Actually, she spent two nights, and in some ways it was even more fun than the wrap party – about which Mum was bursting with curiosity. She couldn't wait to hear all the details, like what sort of restaurant we'd gone to, and what we'd eaten, and what Fawn's parents were like.

"But best keep it between us," she said, when I told her about Fawn's dad being a big-shot businessman and her mum being photographed at Ascot. "Our little secret!"

"Why's that?" whispered Rachel, as we went up to my room.

"It's cos Dad has this thing about St With's being full of rich people," I said. "He thought they might look down on me, or something."

"Like Auntie Helen," said Rachel. "*She* was scared I wouldn't fit in."

"But you have," I said.

Rachel looked at me, eagerly. "Do you really think so?"

I said, "Absolutely! Fawn was so pleased you did the introduction for us."

"I enjoyed it," said Rachel. And then, rather shyly, she added, "Maybe next term, if we have to do more acting, I might be able to take part."

"That would be great," I said.

We were getting there!

We're almost at the end of Year Eight now. Rachel is still called Daffy, by everyone except me. Dodie asked her, once, if she'd rather we called her Rachel, or even Ray, but Rachel said no, she liked being Daffy.

"I know it was cos of my yellow dress that you all hated, but I've kind of got used to it."

Fawn said, "You always wanted to have a nickname."

"She wanted us all to have nicknames," said Tabs. "I remember, on her very first day, she wanted you to be *Baby*."

Dodie giggled. "And she wanted Zoe to be Albatross!"

"I never," protested Rachel. "That was your idea! I wanted her to be Robin."

"We all thought you were totally loopy," said Tabs.

Sometimes, even now, they think that Rachel is a bit odd. It's just that nobody minds any more. As Chantelle recently said, "She may be weird, but she is still One of Us."

It's all she ever wanted. I continue to wait patiently for her to tell me about her life before she came to St With's, which I'm sure she will one day. When she trusts me enough. Danny, meanwhile, is quite forgotten. We never talk about him, and I have never let on that I know the truth. That is something I won't ever do.

Rachel hasn't found herself a real flesh-and-blood boyfriend yet, but then I haven't found myself one, either. We don't worry about it; there are too many other things going on in our lives. Not that we have given up on the idea. I have introduced Rachel to gorgeous Jez, and we both agree that if we should happen to bump into *him* in an Oxfam shop, it would be something to put in our diaries.

"Not," says Rachel, "that we can really expect it."

I am glad she is learning to be realistic where boys are concerned – no more actors! – but I point out that we can always dream. Rachel enthusiastically seconds this.

"There is no harm in just *dreaming*."

"So long as we *know* that it's just dreaming."

"Which we do," says Rachel.

So then we smile at each other and go back to sighing over my poster of Jez. In the meantime, we'd both happily settle for just ordinary regular sorts of boyfriends, such as other people have. All I can say is, we live in hope!

More fantastic reads from Jean Ure...

JELLY BABY

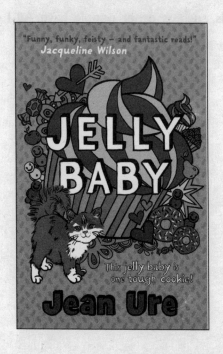

Bitsy, or 'Jelly Baby' as she's sometimes called, has
been doing just fine living with Dad and big sister
Em since Mum died. Until one day Dad brings home
a girlfriend – and everything changes.
Will the Jelly Baby of the family be able to
keep it from falling apart?

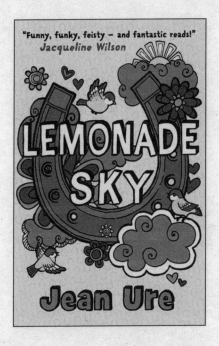

"Funny, funky, feisty – and fantastic reads!"
Jacqueline Wilson

LEMONADE SKY

Jean Ure

When Ruby's mum disappears, Ruby takes
charge – Mum's left her and her two sisters
alone before. But will they be OK? And can
they keep Mum's disappearance a secret until
she gets back?

Salvatore d'Amato is determined to get a kiss by his thirteenth birthday. And not just any kiss. A kiss from his heart's desire – the 'lovely, loveable, luscious Lucy'! With his wonderful love poetry, and his secret body-building, how will she be able to resist? If only that horrible Harmony Hynde would stop bothering him in the meantime!

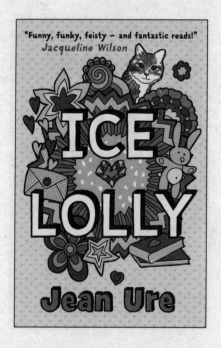

Without Mum, everything is just so *hard*. Things would be easier if I could just stop feeling; if I could just freeze, like an ice lolly...

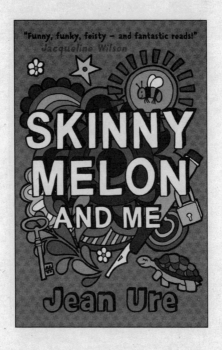

This is the diary of Cherry Louise Waterton.
Problem One: My mum's just remarried a total
dweeb named Roland Butter. Problem Two: I think
she also has a secret too...